CHAPTER 1

MRS. POLLIFAX HAD ATTENDED CHURCH THAT Sunday morning, and her hat—a garden of pale pink roses and green leaves—still sat on her head as she ate lunch in the sunny kitchen of her apartment. She had a tendency to be absent-minded lately about hats—in fact since beginning karate lessons she had become forgetful about a number of things—and since she would be going out again soon she had anticipated the problem by placing her hat where it could not possibly be left behind. This freed her mind for more important matters, such as a review of pressure points, or how to unbalance an assailant with an elbow-upward strike.

But Mrs. Pollifax was conscientious by nature, and if her karate textbook lay to the right of the sugar bowl, the Sunday edition of the *Times* lay on its left. She sighed faintly over her choice but it was the *Times* to which she turned first, carefully unfolding its front page for a quick scanning of the headlines. ENEMY AGENT DEFECTS IN ISTANBUL, THEN VANISHES, she read. *Woman Had Sought Sanctuary in British Consulate, Mysteriously Disappears.*

"Well!" exclaimed Mrs. Pollifax delightedly, and promptly forgot both lunch and karate.

Some months earlier a small episode of espionage had inserted itself like an exclamation point in Mrs. Pollifax's long, serene and unpunctuated life. Once it had ended—and she had enjoyed every moment of it—she had resumed her quiet existence with a sense of enrichment, of having added a dimension to her thoughts that could only be described as a chuckle. That chuckle was present now as she plunged into the news story, for not only was the defecting agent a woman but her past was so lengthy that Mrs. Pollifax guessed that fewer than six years separated them in age.

How very astonishing, she thought, reacting with the fascination of an amateur confronted by her professional counterpart. The news account promised a biography of the woman—Mrs. Pollifax's glance longingly caressed it—but with an exercise of will she saved it for the last.

The woman had leaped into the news by suddenly and mysteriously arriving at the British Consulate in Istanbul, breathless and ragged, to beg for help. After identifying herself as Magda Ferenci-Sabo she had been put to bed at once—at ten o'clock on a summer evening—with a sedative and a cup of tea. In the morning she had vanished, and this was all that the consul—tight-lipped and shaken—allowed himself to say, but rumors swept Istanbul that she had been abducted.

This in itself was front page news, and Mrs. Pollifax eagerly turned to the details of Magda Ferenci-Sabo's life. There were a surprising number, for an enterprising journalist had pieced together a great many old news items, adding suppositions and conclusions that alternately shocked and educated Mrs. Pollifax, who had been a spy quite by accident and for only a few brief weeks. "As an international beauty of the thirties, Ferenci-Sabo appeared at all the right places with the wrong people," commented the author of the article, and there was a blurred picture of her—all teeth and long hair—laughing on a beach with Mussolini. Then there were the marriages: first a French playboy mysteriously killed a year after the honeymoon (the journalist managed to suggest that he had been murdered by his bride); a wealthy German who later became a high official in the Nazi party; and at length a Hungarian Communist writer name Ferenci-Sabo, who was murdered in 1956 by freedom fighters. Following this the woman had disappeared—into Russia, it was believed, where it was rumored that she was actively involved in the INU.

"What an extraordinary woman," mused Mrs. Pollifax;

and obviously a ruthless one as well. She wondered what such a woman thought about when the lovers and husbands had departed, leaving her alone with her thoughts, and she wondered what her motives might be in defecting now. It seemed a curious moment for such a leap. What could possibly have filled her with revulsion *now*?

Reluctantly Mrs. Pollifax put aside both speculations and newspaper because it was—she glanced at the clock on the wall—almost two o'clock of a Sunday afternoon, and before leaving for the Garden Club film (*Gardens of the Mediterranean*) she wanted to compose a grocery list for the week. She reached for pencil and notebook and had just begun to concentrate when the telephone rang. List in hand she walked into the livingroom and before picking up the receiver added EGGS, ORANGE JUICE. "Hello," she said absently, and suddenly remembered that she had promised cookies for the Art Association tea next Sunday.

"Mrs. Pollifax?" said a bright young voice. "Mrs. Emily Pollifax?"

"Speaking," said Mrs. Pollifax, and carefully wrote *sugar*, *vanilla*, *walnuts*.

"One moment please . . ."

A man's voice said, "Good afternoon, Mrs. Pollifax, I'm certainly glad to have found you at home."

The point of Mrs. Pollifax's pencil snapped as she caught her breath sharply. This was a voice that she recognized at once, and a voice she had not expected to hear again. "Why, Mr. Carstairs!" she cried warmly. "How very nice to hear from you!"

"Thank you," he said graciously. "You've been well?"

"Yes—very, thank you."

"Good. I wonder if I might ask two questions of you then that will save us both invaluable time."

"Why not?" said Mrs. Pollifax reasonably. "Except I can't think of anything you don't already know about me."

Carstairs said pleasantly, "I don't know, for instance, if you would be immediately available—or even interested—in doing another job of work for me."

Mrs. Pollifax's heart began to beat very quickly. Split second decisions had never been her forte and she did not want to say yes without first remembering what Mr. Carstairs' work involved but on the other hand if a split second decision was necessary she did not want to say no, either. "Yes," she said recklessly, and promised herself the luxury of thinking about it later.

"Good," said Carstairs. "Question number two: are you free to leave immediately?"

"Immediately?" repeated Mrs. Pollifax, stung by the urgency of the words. "Immediately!" Of course he wasn't serious.

"I can give you thirty minutes."

"To decide whether I can leave immediately?"

"No, to leave."

Mrs. Pollifax was incredulous. Her glance fell to her grocery list, and then moved to the unwashed dishes on the counter in the kitchen; they at least were real. They would also, she remembered, take at least ten minutes to wash and put away. "But where?" she gasped. "For how long?"

Carstairs' voice was patient as if he realized the shock engendered by any such staggering rearrangements of a person's time concepts. "Put it this way," he suggested. "Have you any absolutely vital commitments during the next few days, say between today—Sunday—and Sunday a week?"

"Only my karate lessons," said Mrs. Pollifax. "And then of course I'm to pour at the Art Association tea next Sunday."

"An interesting combination," said Carstairs dryly. "You did say karate?"

"Yes indeed," admitted Mrs. Pollifax with a rush of enthusiasm. "I've been enjoying it enormously and I rather think that Lorvale—retired police sergeant Lorvale Brown—is quite shaken by my success." She stopped, appalled. "What on earth would I *tell* people? How would I explain my—just dashing off?"

"Your daughter-in-law in Chicago will have to be ill," said Carstairs. "We can, for instance, monitor any long distance calls that your son might get from New Brunswick, New Jersey—but that's a problem we'll work out. Count on us."

"Yes," said Mrs. Pollifax, and took a deep breath. "Then I daresay I'd better hang up and get started. I'd better do something. *Something*," she added wanly.

"There will be a police car at your door in precisely

twenty-two minutes. The call went through to them the moment you said yes—"

"How *is* Bishop?" asked Mrs. Pollifax fondly.

"—and in the meantime pack a small bag for a few days of travel. You'll be getting briefed within the hour. And now Godspeed, I leave you with twenty minutes in which to get ready."

"Yes," gasped Mrs. Pollifax, and to her first mental list—knit suit, pink dress—added: cancel newspaper and milk deliveries, notify janitor, Lorvale, Miss Hartshorne . . .

"Goodbye, Mrs. Pollifax," said Carstairs, and abruptly rang off.

Mrs. Pollifax slowly put down the receiver and stared at it. "Well!" she exclaimed softly, reflecting upon how quickly life could change, and then in a surprised voice, *"Well!"* Her gaze fell on the clock and she jumped to her feet and began clearing away the lunch dishes: it gave her something to do. By the time that she had rinsed the dishes there was suddenly a great deal to do. She changed quickly into her navy blue knit suit, immediately placed the flowered hat on her head again, and packed walking shoes, cold cream and travel kit. She telephoned the dairy and then the newsman, and last of all Lorvale.

"I'm off on a little trip, Lorvale," she explained. "My daughter-in-law in Chicago needs me for a few days. I'm terribly sorry but I shall have to miss my Thursday lesson."

"I'm sorry, too," he said reproachfully. "You won't have a chance to practice your omo-tude, will you."

"No, Lorvale," she agreed solemnly.

Her note to Miss Hartshorne was the more difficult because Miss Hartshorne lived across the hall and had met Mrs. Pollifax's son and daughter-in-law at Christmas. The note had to be couched in dramatic enough terms to explain Mrs. Pollifax's precipitous departure—thus canceling a lunch date with her—yet contain just enough information so that Miss Hartshorne would not unduly worry over Roger's wife and telephone Chicago to express her concern.

When the knock came upon her door Mrs. Pollifax was at the telephone again, having nearly forgotten the Art Association tea on Sunday. "Come in, it's unlocked," she called, and turned to nod at the young man who entered her living-room—he was undoubtedly the plainclothes policeman sent by Mr. Carstairs. "It's my taxi," she blandly told the president of the Art Association. "Goodbye, dear."

"You're Mrs. Pollifax?" said the young man as she hung up.

"Yes, and you're—"

"Lieutenant Mullin. The car's outside. This your bag?"

"Oh—thank you." Mrs. Pollifax picked up her purse, hesitated and turned to glance with finality at her dear, familiar apartment. For the first time she allowed herself to compare the world that she was leaving—safe, secure and predictable—with the world she was about to enter, and about the latter she could know nothing at all except that it was certain to prove insecure, difficult and totally unpredictable. "At my age," she murmured doubtfully, and then she recalled that at her age, less than a year ago, she had been held captive in an Albanian prison for a week, and before she led an escape party to the Adriatic those seven days had proven extremely informative and lively: she had met two Red Chinese generals, a Russian spy, and a rogue of an American agent. It was quite unlikely that she would have met them in New Brunswick, New Jersey. It was the quality of a life that mattered, not its quantity, she reflected; and recalling this she straightened her shoulders.

"We're in a hurry," Mullin reminded her.

"Yes," said Mrs. Pollifax, took a deep breath and followed him out into the hall, closing the door firmly behind her. She slipped her note to Miss Hartshorne under the door of apartment 4-C and with this act, at once so final and so irrevocable, all doubts fell from her and she experienced a sudden exhilaration. She had committed herself to another small adventure: something was going to happen.

The elevator door slid open at the first floor, Mullin hastened ahead to hold the outer glass door for her, and they walked into the sticky heat of a July afternoon. The unmarked police car was parked at the curb, next to the No PARKING sign, with a second man at the wheel. Mrs. Pollifax was no sooner seated, with Mullin beside her, when the driver's foot hit the accelerator, a hidden siren began to scream, and Mrs. Pollifax, clinging to her flowered hat, was startled into delight. How marvelous to be involved in so much haste, she thought, and was not even dismayed when she found herself suddenly gazing into the eyes of her astonished pastor, who barely escaped the racing car by jumping back to the curb. *"C'est la vie,"* she called out gaily, fluttering her hand at him, and then they were leaving the city behind, cars scattering to right and left at the sound of the siren. Moments later they entered the gates of the small local airport. The police car bounced across the field and came to a screaming halt in front of a helicopter whose blades were already beating the air. Mrs. Pollifax, clinging desperately to her hat now, was boosted into the copter, and almost before she had reworked her hatpins the helicopter was landing at a very busy and much larger airfield.

They appeared to be expected: a man in a wrinkled beige suit left a waiting car and raced toward them. "Mrs. Pollifax?" he shouted up at her.

"Yes," she screamed back, and was dropped from the cockpit into his arms.

"Over here," he said, grasping her elbow. "They're holding the plane. Jamison's my name."

"Yes, but where am I going?" she gasped.

"Later." He hurried her into the car, which immediately tore off with a squeal of tires.

"Then where am I now?" demanded Mrs. Pollifax.

"Kennedy International," he told her. "You did very well time-wise, but that plane over there is waiting just for us and they've already held up the flight five minutes."

"Flight for where?" asked Mrs. Pollifax again.

"Washington. Carstairs wants to brief you personally before you leave the country."

So she was to leave the country; Mrs. Pollifax felt that shiver of the irrevocable again, of forces in motion that could no longer be halted, and then the reaction passed as swiftly as it had arrived. The car stopped, the door was thrown open and Mrs. Pollifax was hurried up steps and into the plane, where she and Jamison were belted into their seats at once. Before Mrs. Pollifax had sufficiently caught her breath they were landing again.

"Dulles Airport," contributed Jamison with authority, and once they had reached the terminal he guided her through the building to the parking area. "Here we are," he said, pointing to a long black limousine, and from it emerged Carstairs, tall, thin, his shock of crew-cut hair pure white against his tanned face.

"Good afternoon, Mrs. Pollifax," he said gravely, as if they had met only yesterday and she had not been spirited to his side in less than an hour.

"I'm delighted to see you," said Mrs. Pollifax, clasping his hand warmly. "It's seemed such a long time. How have things been going?"

Carstairs said cheerfully, "Abominably, as always." He gestured toward a stolid-looking young man in a dark suit and black tie. "I'd like you to meet Henry Miles first."

"How do you do," said Mrs. Pollifax politely.

"Henry is going to be traveling behind you but not with you, and it's important you know what the other looks like."

"Behind me?" echoed Mrs. Pollifax as they shook hands.

"He's keeping an eye on you," explained Carstairs, and added with a faint smile, "This time I'm taking no chances with you. All right, Jamison, take Henry off to seat 22 and make sure that plane doesn't get away!" To Mrs. Pollifax he said, "You're about to depart for the Near East. Come and sit in my car, we've only fifteen minutes in which to talk."

CHAPTER 2

"THE NEAR EAST!" ECHOED MRS. POLLIFAX. "Yes, on a ticklish courier assignment, and a risky one, the necessity of which became obvious only thirty minutes before I telephoned you." They were seated now in the rear of the limousine and he brought his attaché case to his lap. "I'm sending you to Istanbul," he said.

"Istanbul!" exclaimed Mrs. Pollifax, and in an astonished voice added, "Do you know, I was reading a news story from Istanbul only a few minutes before you telephoned!" She looked at him doubtfully. "Are you—that is, does this have anything to do with the Ferenci-Sabo woman, the Communist spy who tried to defect?"

"A great deal to do with it," Carstairs said. He unzipped the attaché case to expose an interior bulging with papers. Glancing up at her he said, "Except that rather a lot has happened since that news story you read."

"She's been found?" said Mrs. Pollifax eagerly.

"No." He shook his head. "If you take a second look at the dateline on your news story you'll discover the story was held up for twenty-four hours—Ferenci-Sabo reached the consulate Friday night, God knows how, and was taken in. No, she's not been found. This is Sunday afternoon—already late evening in Istanbul because of the time difference—and during these hours Istanbul has turned into a hotbed of intrigue, with agents pouring into the city from every point of the globe, all with one hope: either to find Ferenci-Sabo and

9

offer her sanctuary in their country, or find Ferenci-Sabo and silence her, depending upon their political stance."

"She really was abducted then," said Mrs. Pollifax. "I thought—because of her importance—she might have been hidden away somewhere by the British."

"She was abducted all right," Carstairs said grimly. "Very cleverly, too, and it's believed she was abducted by Communists. The curious point is that she was abducted and not murdered. If it was silence her captors wanted, they need only have killed her in her bed at the consulate—the devils seemed to have had no problem entering the building! It leaves the implication that Ferenci-Sabo still has more value alive than dead—a conclusion," he added dryly, "that many other intelligence agencies have also reached. Ferenci-Sabo has now become fair game for everybody—and a great number of ruthless people have entered the game. A woman of Ferenci-Sabo's background was bound to be coveted but since she's been abducted, and is presumably still in Istanbul, there are high hopes that what one country has accomplished can be neatly done by another."

"I see," said Mrs. Pollifax, and waited patiently for the explanation that might make some sense of her being here. At the moment she could see no light at all.

As if reading her thoughts he said gravely, "I've called upon you, Mrs. Pollifax—with Miles to keep an eye on you—because in a city teeming with professionals you lack the slightest aura of corruption or professionalism yet at the same time"—his mouth curved wryly—"at the same time you give every evidence of being a resourceful courier."

"Thank you," said Mrs. Pollifax, "but a courier for what? I don't understand."

He said quietly. "We have heard from Ferenci-Sabo."

"You?" she said in astonishment. "The CIA? But how? When? Why?"

He held up his hand. "Please, we know almost nothing except that in a situation where we're technically only innocent bystanders we suddenly find ourselves in the position of being like the recipient of a ransom note in a kidnap case. No, that's misleading: she's apparently eluded her kidnappers and is alive and in hiding in Istanbul."

"How incredible," said Mrs. Pollifax.

He nodded. "The message, received late this morning, said only that Ferenci-Sabo would go each evening at eight o'clock to the lobby of the Hotel Itep—a small Turkish hotel in the old section—and look for someone carrying a copy of *Gone with the Wind*."

"*Gone with the Wind!*" echoed Mrs. Pollifax, suppressing a laugh.

"In Istanbul it's now almost Sunday midnight," went on Carstairs. "We had time to immediately notify our agent in Istanbul, who presented himself at eight o'clock at the Hotel Itep." Carstairs' mouth tightened. "Word of his death reached us thirty minutes before I telephoned you, Mrs. Pollifax. I *cannot* regard it as an accident."

Mrs. Pollifax expelled her breath slowly. "Oh," she said soberly. "Oh dear!"

"Yes. At eight-fifteen he walked out of the hotel with a woman companion—and a car suddenly went berserk in the street, pinning him to the wall and killing him instantly. The woman seen with him vanished into the crowd."

"I'm terribly sorry," Mrs. Pollifax said. "You think he met Ferenci-Sabo there?"

Carstairs shrugged. "It's quite possible, in which case she must be even more desperate after seeing her contact killed before her very eyes. You are in effect replacing a dead man, Mrs. Pollifax—but with one difference."

"Yes?"

"There may be a leak somewhere—or with so damn many agents in Istanbul they may be keeping one another under surveillance—but no one could possibly recognize you, or suspect you of being an agent. I intend that no one outside of this building know of your departure. In the world of espionage there are only two living people who have ever met you—John Sebastian Farrell, currently in South America, and General Perdido, now recovering from a heart attack in Peking. And this is the way I plan to keep it. Henry Miles knows nothing except that you are to be kept under surveillance—I'm sure that not even in his wildest dreams would he guess that a novice is being sent into such a maelstrom, even if he should know the situation—which he doesn't. In turn you are to send no cables nor contact me at all. You are to trust no one and above all," he concluded grimly, "you're to watch for reckless drivers when crossing streets in Istanbul. Now I think you will be happy to learn that this time you travel with a passport—a bona fide one accomplished for you in an hour's time."

"How nice," said Mrs. Pollifax, as he handed it to her. "Even my photograph!"

"Yes, we took one for our files, you may remember."

"Very efficient."

"Also money," he said, drawing a manila envelope from the attaché case and handing it to her. "Rather a lot of money because of the unpredictability of the—er—situation. And in this second envelope is money for Ferenci-Sabo, as well as a passport for her in another name. It lacks a photograph, of course, and this she will have to supply but it has all the necessary stampings proving that she entered Turkey legally a week ago, and as an American citizen. Here are your plane tickets," he added, "as well as an especially gaudy edition of *Gone with the Wind*. A reservation has been made for you at the Hotel Itep—there wasn't time to be devious— and Henry Miles will have a room there too, but you are to avoid Henry, you understand? I don't want you linked with a professional under any circumstances—we've already lost one. And on Saturday morning you are to fly back whether you have made contact or not."

"All the way to Asia and back in six days?" said Mrs. Pollifax. "My dear Mr. Carstairs I shall almost be back in time for the Art Association tea on Sunday."

"As a matter of fact by American time you will be," he said. "You will experience the uncanny sensation of arriving here long after the tea should have ended, only to discover that they're putting up the folding tables in New Brunswick. Ah here it is!" he exclaimed, and drew out another slip of paper. "I can't foresee what will be needed, Mrs. Pollifax. All this has happened too quickly to consider possibilities, but I'm giving you the name of a man in Istanbul who can be trusted in case of emergency. He's lived in Istanbul for a number of years, and you can rely on him to advise and help—but only if you have absolutely no other recourse. He's very highly placed so for God's sake be discreet if you go to him."

"An agent?" inquired Mrs. Pollifax cheerfully.

Carstairs looked pained. "My dear Mrs. Pollifax, I do wish you'd not leap to such dramatic conclusions. He's a noted criminologist, retired now, who writes and teaches. His name is Dr. Guillaume Belleaux. You will find the name of the university with which he is connected on this slip of paper, as well as his home address. There's no need to destroy or hide this address, Dr. Belleaux is highly respected by the Turkish government as well as ours, and any tourist might legitimately carry his name. Now." He smiled. "Got it all?"

Mrs. Pollifax was stuffing the envelopes into her fat purse. The book she placed under her arm. "I'm to register at the Hotel Itep," she said, "and to present myself in the lobby at eight each evening until—hopefully—Ferenci-Sabo appears; I'm to give her passport and money, remember the name of Dr. Belleaux, and help Ferenci-Sabo in whatever way is needed."

"Right—and then vanish." Carstairs glanced quickly at his watch. "Now before we wrap this up are there questions?"

"Yes." She said slowly, "You say there may be a leak somewhere, Mr. Carstairs. You've also—somehow and very mysteriously—set up a meeting with a woman who is a notorious Communist agent." She hesitated. "Yet nobody has seen her, and your Istanbul agent was killed trying to meet her." She looked at him. "Don't you suspect a trap? Do you really trust this woman?"

Carstairs smiled faintly. "Quite true, Mrs. Pollifax, and this is why I insisted on briefing you personally." He removed a slip of yellow paper from the attaché case and handed it to her. "This is how we were advised about the rendezvous at the Hotel Itep."

Mrs. Pollifax took the proffered paper and read:

ISTANBUL: ARRIVED AT SIX STOP HAVE ENJOYED EIGHT HOURS ITEP OTELI STOP WISH YOU COULD JOIN ME STOP WHY NOT SEND RED QUEEN OR BLACK JACK BEFORE FRIDAY STOP LOVE ALICE DEXTER WHITE.

Mrs. Pollifax frowned. "Should I know what this means?"

Carstairs laughed. "On the contrary it took the coding department a number of trips to the archives to identify it and I don't believe they would have decoded it yet if the names of

Red Queen and Black Jack hadn't been included. This was a code—a very simple one invented for rendezvous purposes— used by a small group of agents working in Occupied Paris during World War Two."

"World War Two," echoed Mrs. Pollifax, utterly lost. "But this has the flavor of a period piece!"

"Exactly. Code 6—this one, if you note the time of arrival— automatically stood for rendezvousing in a hotel lobby, with a copy of *Gone with the Wind* if identification was neces- sary. Code 5 stood for a metro station—I believe a Bible was used there—and seven, if I remember correctly, meant a church, and always the seventh pew on the left. And so on— there were eight in all. Red Queen was an agent named Agatha Simms, unfortunately killed several years ago in Hong Kong, and Black Jack was the code name of another agent in that group."

"And Alice Dexter White?" asked Mrs. Pollifax.

Carstairs looked at her and then he looked down at the unlighted cigarette he held. "A very dear friend of mine which is how I come into this," he said quietly. "A very re- markable woman to whom I twice owe my life, and with whom I worked during those war years." He lifted his glance and regarded her with level eyes. "You are now about to join a very small and exclusive club, Mrs. Pollifax—only four living people know what I am about to tell you." He tapped the yellow cable with a finger. "This woman is one of our most valued agents but Alice Dexter White is only her code name. Her real name is Magda Ferenci-Sabo."

Mrs. Pollifax caught her breath sharply. "Good heavens," she gasped, "but this turns everything upside down!"

CHAPTER 3

 DURING THE FIRST HOUR OF HER TRANSATLANTIC
flight Mrs. Pollifax had time to consider the events
of the afternoon, but she was not at all certain that
this was to her advantage. Her head still spun from her
briefing with Carstairs, and it was difficult to find some
graspable point of view with which to organize all that he
had told her. "You remain, principally, a courier," he had
said, "because I'm working on the assumption that once she
has passport and money Ferenci-Sabo will know what to do.
You may be called upon to help with a disguise, but she
should be able to manage the rest herself. If by any chance it
proves too hot for her to leave the country legally, this is
when I recommend your approaching Dr. Belleaux."

"Why did she use such an ancient code?" Mrs. Pollifax
had asked, understanding better now the choice of *Gone
with the Wind*.

"Probably it's the only one she could recall from
memory," he'd said. "Codes were simpler, more primitive,
then. In those days she was Frau Wetzelmann," he added
reminiscently.

"And you were Black Jack," guessed Mrs. Pollifax.

"Yes," he said quietly, and then, "Mrs. Pollifax, we don't
know why Ferenci-Sabo came to Istanbul, or how, but this is
one 'notorious Communist agent,' who must be allowed to
defect. Must," he emphasized fiercely. "Not only for her

sake—and what we owe her—but for ours as well, because
if ever she were forced to talk—" He shuddered.

Mrs. Pollifax shivered a little too now, and opened up
the copy of *House Beautiful* on her lap. Up and down the
aisle passengers were studiously reading about the woman
that Mrs. Pollifax was en route to meet. What was even
more unnerving she now knew a great deal more about
Ferenci-Sabo than the New York *Times*, and this in itself
awed Mrs. Pollifax. But on the whole, as material for re-
flection, it was all too overwhelming and after a while Mrs.
Pollifax sensibly decided to stop thinking about it. Since
by European time she would not arrive in Istanbul until
late tomorrow afternoon she closed her eyes and presently
slept.

Monday's dawn had arrived when they reached London,
and as Mrs. Pollifax disembarked from the plane she set her
watch ahead, noting that at home she would be listening to
the eleven o'clock news before retiring for the night—how
very odd traveling was! After purchasing a small travel
guide to Turkey she made her way into the waiting room to
await the departure of her plane to Istanbul. She noticed that
Henry Miles wandered about for a little while and then
found a seat nearby, sat down and lighted a cigarette. They
exchanged impersonal glances and then Miles endeared
himself to Mrs. Pollifax by slowly, wickedly closing one
eyelid and winking at her. Until that wink he had appeared
curiously invisible, totally lacking in personality and con-
tent, as if he drew himself in flat chalk and then erased
all but the outline. Now Mrs. Pollifax realized that a
second Henry Miles walked, sat, stood and breathed inside
that first Henry Miles, although a few seconds later, her
glance returning, it was impossible to believe in that other
personage, he looked so buttoned-up again.

The flight to Istanbul was announced, and Mrs. Pollifax
boarded the plane and took her seat near the wing, with
Miles several rows in front of her. This time she acquired a
seat companion, and one who arrived breathlessly, with
every male including Henry turning his head to stare at
her. Mrs. Pollifax stared, too—she had never seen anyone
quite like her before, which made the encounter educa-
tional as well. The girl was very young; she was dressed

in an incredible outfit of dramatic greens and purples crowned with a brilliant green stovepipe hat which she removed almost at once, displaying a flawless profile. Her eyelids and her lips had been painted white, her long eyelashes were ink black, and she wore her straight red-gold hair to the waist. Once she had settled her bag and her magazines she turned to look at Mrs. Pollifax with equal interest, gazed frankly at the wisps of hair escaping Mrs. Pollifax's flowered hat, met her admiring and startled glance and smiled.

"Hello," she said, adding with a burst of candor. "Do I frighten you? I do some of my mother's friends—not that Mother has many pious friends but she does have tons of pious acquaintances, Daddy being an M.P."

"Parliament!" said Mrs. Pollifax rapturously.

"You're American!" exclaimed the girl. "What fun! Yes, Daddy's in Parliament, and I've just become a model, isn't it wonderful? It's terribly exciting. I hope to be an actress, but I think modeling's a marv way to begin. I'm on my way to Athens for a job. Tony and the cameras are already there— they're doing me in autumn clothes against the Acropolis and all that."

"Oh yes," said Mrs. Pollifax, beaming, and then, "I'd forgotten we stop at Athens. I'm going all the way through to Istanbul."

The girl's face lit up. "I say, that's wonderful! My brother's there. If I've time after the assignment I'm hoping to fly over and see him." A faint shadow dimmed her preposterously radiant face. "At least I hope he's still there," she added darkly. "He has such an awful time with just—well, just the *mechanics* of living. It's unbelievable." She sighed and tucked her young chin in the palm of her hand.

"What does he do in Istanbul?" asked Mrs. Pollifax, intrigued by her concern.

"Well, he's been given a job with Uncle Hubert," she explained. "But of course you wouldn't know what that means unless you knew my family. It means, translated, that everybody's simply given up on Colin—my brother—and nobody knows what else to do with him." She frowned. "I suppose every large family has one."

"One what?" asked Mrs. Pollifax.

The girl hesitated, and then said angrily, "Somebody who just doesn't fit, you know? And that person knows it and grows up—well, grows up feeling *invisible*. And it turns into a vicious circle because it's so desperately easy not to notice someone invisible, but nobody understands this."

Mrs. Pollifax smiled faintly. She decided she liked this girl. "You're fond of him then. But being fond is a form of understanding."

"Oh I understand what's wrong," the girl said earnestly. "But not how to help. Colin has no confidence, just no confidence at all, and because of this he absolutely bristles with hostility. He's gotten battered, you know? He's very precise by nature but he can't find anything to be precise about, if you know what I mean, and this is infuriating for him and he loathes himself. But although I understand all this I'm very bad for him because he brings out the maternal in me. I'm a Moon Child, you see—born under the sign of Cancer, and simply seething with motherly instincts. He hates that. Quite rightly, too—he's terribly intelligent, of course. Oh I do hope I'll have time to stop and see him, but I despair," she explained dramatically. "There's never enough time. It'll rain, and the filming get held up for days—things always happen like that in this business."

"You could write to your brother then," suggested Mrs. Pollifax comfortingly.

The girl turned her head and stared wonderingly at Mrs. Pollifax. "Write?" she repeated blankly, and Mrs. Pollifax understood that she had stumbled upon a word utterly foreign to this girl and her generation.

"It's a way to keep in touch."

"In touch," repeated the girl musingly. "Yes, we do rocket about a great deal, my friends and I. But still I know what you mean. I think 'in touch' is a beautiful expression, don't you? And yet I do feel in touch with Colin always, even when I never see him."

"Then you have something very rare and wonderful," pointed out Mrs. Pollifax. "A bond."

The girl nodded, beaming now. "You do see it, don't you. But what takes you to Istanbul, and why Istanbul?"

Why indeed, thought Mrs. Pollifax, and announced that she was going to do a little sightseeing, and also meet a friend there. "An old friend who has been exploring the Middle East," she added firmly.

"But that's marv," said the girl. "Oh I do wonder if—how long will you be in Istanbul?"

"Until Saturday morning," said Mrs. Pollifax calmly. "I wonder if I can guess what you're thinking."

The girl laughed delightedly. "Of course you can because you're a dear, I can tell, and probably psychic as well. But you know, Colin just *might* be useful to you, having been in Istanbul for four months. And if I shouldn't have the time to fly over to see him—it's vital Colin feel that somebody cares—"

"Being a Moon Child," said Mrs. Pollifax gravely.

"Well, I truly can't help it, can I? And nobody else cares, not really, except in a generalized family sense, and only when something goes hideously *wrong*, if you know what I mean. Of course I shouldn't want to burden you—"

Mrs. Pollifax smiled. "If you'll give me his address I'll try. I can't promise anything but there might be time."

"Oh you *are* a dear," the girl said, and removing a ring from her finger handed it to Mrs. Pollifax. "Give him this, that's the important thing. It's his, really, he gave it to me when he left. It's a game we've played for years, handing it back and forth for luck. I wore it when he went off to Oxford—except he flunked out," she explained with a sigh. "Then he wore it when he sold vacuum cleaners—but Mother was the only one who bought one—and then he sold encyclopedias, or did he work at Fortnum's next? Oh brother I can't remember. Anyway, give him this and my love."

"But this is a valuable signet ring," pointed out Mrs. Pollifax. "And really there may be no time at all—"

"Then you can just tuck it into an envelope and mail it back to me—I'll give you my address as well," she said. She had begun laboriously printing on a sheet of memo with a small address book propped on her knee. When she handed it to Mrs. Pollifax it read:

COLIN RAMSEY,
RAMSEY ENTERPRISES LTD.
23 ZIKZAK DAR SOKAK, STAMBOUL.

* * *

To this she had added,

> MISS MIA RAMSEY
> C/O HEATHERTON AGENCY,
> PICCADILLY CIRCUS, LONDON W.I

"And I am Emily Pollifax," said Mrs. Pollifax, feeling that introductions were being made, if half of them on paper. "Also a Moon Child," she added with a twinkle.

"No! Are you really?" demanded Mia breathlessly. "Then that's what I felt at once. Colin's Capricorn, you know, that's why he's so inherently precise."

"My husband was a Libra," put in Mrs. Pollifax.

"But how marv," breathed the girl. "Charm? Diplomacy? Harmony?"

"Oh yes," said Mrs. Pollifax, nodding.

"Most of my family's Gemini," Mia added broodingly. "A very restless sign to be born under, you know. Tony's Libra," she confided. "He wants to marry me."

"Tony?"

"The man in charge of all this," she said with a sweeping gesture that apparently included her outrageous costume. "The one waiting for me in Athens. He's a marv photographer."

"And do you love him?" asked Mrs. Pollifax with interest.

Mia turned thoughtful. "I'm only eighteen, you know. Do you think it possible to love at eighteen?"

"In general no," said Mrs. Pollifax.

Mia nodded. "That's what I think, too. It's tempting—and terribly romantic—but I do want to find out who I am first. I don't want to be married umpteen times. It's so unstable."

At this point they were interrupted by lunch—the meals were growing very confusing—and then they were nearing Athens, and Mrs. Pollifax watched Mia reline her lips and eyelids with white, and comb her long hair. As the plane touched earth and taxied down the runway Mia looked at Mrs. Pollifax with huge eyes. "Do you realize we may never meet again?" she said in dismay, and was suddenly a very young child.

Mrs. Pollifax smiled. "But it's so very nice that we've met at all," she said warmly.

Mia laughed. "There I go, being greedy again—you're much the wiser." Standing, she leaned over and impulsively kissed Mrs. Pollifax on the cheek. "God bless," she said warmly, and placing her stovepipe hat securely on the top of her head she walked down the aisle, every eye on the plane fastened just as securely upon her receding figure.

Mrs. Pollifax watched her go. She thought she left behind her a very definite fragrance—not of an orchid in spite of her exotic green and purple appearance, she reflected, but something rather sturdy and British, like a primrose. Yes, a primrose, decided Mrs. Pollifax, and with a little smile brought out her travel guide on Turkey again, and settled down to read it.

CHAPTER 4

MRS. POLLIFAX LANDED AT AN AIRPORT WHOSE name she could not pronounce, and went through Customs in a state of numbness. Not even a glimpse of her first mosque or the delicate spire of a minaret roused her from this alarming sense of detachment; she was experiencing now the effect of crossing two continents and an ocean in the space of a day. She remembered that she had been contacted by Carstairs at two o'clock on a quiet Sunday afternoon, she had left the United States less than two hours later, and she had been in flight for seventeen hours, with a brief stopover in London. In America it would be Monday morning and she would be preparing to shop at the A&P, but instead she was in Istanbul and it was four o'clock Monday afternoon, all of which produced a bewildered weightless and unattached feeling: it was difficult to realize that she had reached Istanbul, or how, or for what purpose. As the airline bus carried her toward the city there was added to her blurredness a steady cacophony of noise: horns honking, donkeys braying, and vendors shouting.

When Mrs. Pollifax reached the Oteli Itep and registered at the desk, showing her passport, it was five o'clock. There was no sign of Henry, which reminded her that they were in Istanbul now and there would be no more reassuring winks. The desk clerk himself showed her to her room on the second floor and left her staring, mesmerized, at the bed.

And the bed really was enchanting. It was mounted on a

22

platform that made it the focal point of the room, it was covered with a brilliant scarlet afghan and what was more it looked voluptuously soft. Mrs. Pollifax moved toward it with longing, every bone of her body still in protest against the reclining seats into which she had been fitted for so long. She reached up to her flowered hat, fumbled for its hatpin and then hesitated. She remembered that in fewer than three hours she must take up her post in the lobby with her copy of *Gone with the Wind*—it was why she was here—and by that hour she must be alert and rested. She had already done a great deal of sleeping on the plane, and another nap could only leave her woolly-headed. A more sensible idea would be to find something to occupy and clear her mind. She thought of food but she was not hungry enough to spend the next hour in dining, and in any case she would prefer breakfast to dinner, her appetite being still on American time. Yet somehow before eight o'clock she had to recover a degree of perception and awareness, and enough vitality to think clearly.

"A walk!" she thought. "A good brisk walk!" It was the perfect idea, jewel-like in its simplicity and wisdom after so many hours of tedium. She wondered if the bazaars would be open at this hour, doubted, and immediately suffered a loss of motivation until she remembered Mia Ramsey's brother.

"What a very nice idea, and it shouldn't take long!" she exclaimed aloud, and at once felt a leap of interest and purpose. She dug the brother's address out of her purse, noted that they were both in the old part of the city but decided nevertheless to take a taxi there and do her walking on the way back.

Washing her face in very cold water she left the room without opening her suitcase, walked down the heavily carpeted stairs to the lobby, nodded cheerfully to the desk clerk and strolled out into the bustling life of the streets.

According to her map Istanbul was a city divided by bridges, water and the geographical coincidence of existing upon two continents, Europe and Asia. Mrs. Pollifax assessed the character of it with a certain feminine casualness: the newer section, called Beyoglu, contained the Hilton Istanbul, and therefore must also contain the newer residences, the higher priced hotels, and most of the tourists. The older section, called Stamboul, appeared to hold most of the minarets, mosques, bazaars, native hotels as well as herself and Mia Ramsey's brother. With this settled she hailed a taxi. The driver greeted her effusively, swore by Allah that Zikzak was not far, that his taxi was the best in Stamboul, he was a fine driver and it was a beautiful evening, and they started out.

Delighted by her resourcefulness and already reviving at the thought of exchanging words with an authentic resident of the city, Mrs. Pollifax sat back in anticipation. What struck her forcibly as she looked around her was the patina of antiquity everywhere that went beyond old age; there was a grandeur in the shabbiness of Stamboul's flaking walls, peeling stucco, faded paint and eroded columns. It rested the eye: this city was thousands of years old. Istanbul also impressed her now as being a surprisingly gay place, and her ears began to sort out the sounds that had dismayed her earlier. A great deal of commerce appeared to be transacted from the sides and backs of donkeys, upon which were carried baskets of flowers, bread, tinware, bales of cloth, jugs of water, herbs and sweets, all of which had to be advertised incessantly and vocally, the louder the better. Children played and shouted. Strange weird music drifted out of shuttered windows and open doors. The light itself was purest Mediterranean—why had she assumed Istanbul would be gloomy?—and as they drove up and down unbelievably steep streets Mrs. Pollifax was reminded of San Francisco.

But gradually the streets grew narrower, darker and less traveled, and Mrs. Pollifax began to experience a growing sense of alarm. After all, they were in search of a business called Ramsey Enterprises Ltd., which had a solid, respectable and undeniably British ring to it, whereas this was old Istanbul, and growing older and older at each turn. For the first time she remembered the two envelopes in her purse, each of them bulging with money, and when the taxi turned into a cul-de-sac, a dead end alley with a high wall running along one side, Mrs. Pollifax was certain that she was going to be held up and robbed. She was wondering if she dared try out her karate—and which blow to deliver—when the driver brought the cab to a stop, jerked his head toward a ramshackle building on the left which leaned precariously to one side, and turning to her said, "Twenty-three Zikzak."

"Are you sure?" she asked doubtfully. She handed the printed address to the driver for verification.

"Evet, evet," he said, nodding indignantly, and jumped out and opened the door for her.

Mrs. Pollifax climbed out, paid the man—or over-paid him, she reflected wryly, having still no firm grasp of the country's lira and kurush—and when she walked across the alley to the lopsided door experienced the small shock of relief at discovering all her suspicions unfounded. The man was reliable and she was indeed in the correct place. But what an astonishingly unprepossessing place it was! A neat sign over the bell said RAMSEY ENTERPRISES LTD. A small dusty sign below it read RAMSEY DOCUMENTARIES IN REAR (Documentaries! thought Mrs. Pollifax); a third sign read HUBERT LUDLOW RAMSEY, ESQ. Mrs. Pollifax pushed the bell. Nothing happened. Sounds of traffic came dimly to her ears, and among the wilting bougainvillea a bee droned monotonously. From the other side of the alley's wall came shouts of muffled argument, and from a distance the sound of a muezzin's chant. Mrs. Pollifax turned her back on the front door and walked firmly down the narrow, beaten-earth driveway toward RAMSEY DOCUMENTARIES IN REAR.

She came out upon a small cobbled courtyard walled with bougainvillea. A dusty van was parked here beside an equally dusty old jeep, and beyond them lay a series of small cement-block buildings, obviously quite new: a garage, a building with two skylights, and a small office bearing a sign RAMSEY ENTERPRISES. The door to this office stood open, and as Mrs. Pollifax approached it she heard someone swearing—steadily and scathingly—in English.

"Good afternoon," called out Mrs. Pollifax cheerfully.

The swearing immediately broke off, and a round, owlish face peered around the door. "What the devil!" exclaimed the young man in baffled astonishment, and then, "I say— I'm awfully sorry, you overheard the swearing?"

"Every word," said Mrs. Pollifax amiably. "Is it a habit of yours?"

"It's rapidly becoming one," he said crossly from some-where inside ("I'm putting on a shirt," he explained in an aside). "I'm swearing because I've been doing some filming while my uncle's away and not one damned frame has come out yet. My uncle will have my head for it. No, he'll proba-bly fire me."

"Why didn't the pictures come out?" inquired Mrs. Polli-fax curiously.

His voice drew closer. "Because yesterday I left the lens cap on, and today they're all light-struck." He suddenly ap-peared in the door, a small, compact young man wearing a fierce scowl, dusty khaki shorts, dusty shirt and dusty boots.

"Then you must be Colin Ramsey," said Mrs. Pollifax warmly, extending her hand. "You have to be Colin Ramsey."

"I don't have to be but I am," he said suspiciously. "Are you a friend of Uncle Hu's?"

"No, of your sister's," she told him. "That is, I flew from London to Athens with her today—my name's Mrs. Pollifax—and if I had time she asked me to stop in and give you both her love and this ring."

His face brightened. "Did she really! I say, that's decent of her." He took the ring and looked at it. "Beautiful Mia—what on earth is she doing in Athens! I suppose she's left school again?"

"I didn't hear anything about school; she's modeling."

He nodded, still staring down at the ring. "Funny," he mused, "this came from Uncle Hu when we were still in the nursery, I'd forgotten its source until this minute. He gave it me, said it was magic or some such bit of whimsy, and for years I wore it faithfully on a string around my neck. That's how it all started, and here I am working for Uncle Hu now, and the ring's here, too." His laugh was so bitter it startled him as well as Mrs. Pollifax and he glanced up. "It's really decent of you to have bothered with this, and I'm being ter-ribly rude, boring you with my blighted life. May I offer you a lemonade?"

"You weren't being rude, you were feeling sorry for your-self," pointed out Mrs. Pollifax firmly. "And yes it *was* de-cent of me, except that I had too much time for just eating and not enough time for sleeping because of having to be back at the hotel before eight. Also I was curious. Yes, I will have a lemonade, thank you."

"Curious because of Mia?" he asked.

"Not entirely. I thought it restful—soothing, you know— to have a small errand to run, and the name and address of someone here, in a strange city and strange country." She stopped and suddenly smiled. "It just occurs to me: I'm probably feeling a touch of homesickness. Or rather of not-at-homeness."

He nodded. "Your first trip abroad?"

Mrs. Pollifax smiled faintly. "Yes and no," she said adroitly. "The first alone, at least."

"Then do come and have that lemonade," he suggested understandingly. "Although if you're traveling alone who's the chap with you, your driver? Guide?"

Mrs. Pollifax looked at him blankly. "There's no one with me. I came in a taxi but the driver went away." She turned, following Colin's glance up the driveway to the alley. "What is it?"

He grinned. "Some tourist—a chap in a dark suit with a camera. He's strolled past twice, trying not to look too interested in us. Tourists don't usually get this far."

Henry, thought Mrs. Pollifax warmly. But how absolutely astute of him, she reflected, he had not for a moment forsaken his post, he had seen her leave and followed. A rush of gratitude flooded her at such touching protectiveness, and then she put the thought aside and turned and followed Colin toward the house. "But how do you happen to notice such things?" she asked of Colin, responding at once to such an active imagination.

He smiled ruefully as he held open the door to the house. "Compensation, I guess—observation is my only talent. I'm a complete embarrassment to a brilliant family—it's why they've shipped me out here to Turkey."

Mrs. Pollifax entered a bleak, cheerless kitchen dominated by a very old refrigerator with coils on the top. "Purest Soho, circa 1920," commented Colin with a gesture toward the room. "Do have a seat."

Mrs. Pollifax slid gratefully onto a bench beside a long trestle table. "But what kind of brilliant family?" she asked. "That is, if you could use just one word—"

"That's easy," said Colin, removing ice cube trays from the antique refrigerator. "Successful."

Mrs. Pollifax nodded. "But in what way? What values?"

He scowled. "Well, they climb mountains. Big ones," he added angrily. "They excel at rugby and take honors at Oxford and rather tend to get knighted. They go into the Army and win medals, that sort of thing. My father's an M.P. My two brothers went to Sandhurst and they'll either be generals or M.P.s, wait and see. You met my sister. She's the baby of the family, but if she's taken up modeling she'll be a top model on all the magazine covers by Christmas. My mother's a poet and the last time I saw a London *Times* she was in jail for picketing—some kind of labor protest. That's being a success these days too, you know." He gloomily handed Mrs. Pollifax a frosty glass of lemonade and sat down across the table from her.

Mrs. Pollifax said tartly, "I think someone in your family read far too much Halliburton in their youth. But if they're active and extroverted and like heights, that's their prerogative. What do *you* like best?"

He looked thoughtful. "It's hard to say, you know. I'm an absolute physical coward. I daresay that's something most people don't have to learn about themselves by the age of eight, but living with my family I learned it early. Alpine climbing absolutely terrifies me, boxing appalls me and fencing scares the hell out of me. The Army didn't turn out to be my cup of tea and I flunked out of Oxford." He brightened. "Frankly I like it *here*. It's a joy having nobody care that I'm a Ramsey, and Uncle Hu doesn't care tuppence about climbing mountains, he's too busy running this rum outfit. But damn it I'm desperately afraid that just when I've found the right nook I shall blow it. Failure *can* get to be a habit, you know."

"Nonsense," put in Mrs. Pollifax flatly.

"But just see what's happened. Uncle Hu goes off to Erzurum with his projection man for a week, and after showing me the work for four months he leaves me with just ten minutes of filming, the first assignment he's given me, and I'm already blowing the whole thing. He runs a shoestring operation; I ask you, how long can he afford me?"

Mrs. Pollifax glanced curiously around the barren room.

"You mean this address is all there is to Ramsey Enterprises Ltd.?"

Colin nodded. "Mostly it's a matter of traveling around the country—he comes back here to splice and develop film and pick up his mail. He has a tie-in with the British Council. Winters he puts chains and a snowplow on the van and goes on tour, as he calls it. Shows Turkish films in the *hata series*—the council houses in the villages—and occasionally shows films from England. There are thousands of little villages in Turkey and for some of them it's the only contact they have with the outside world except for the traveling schoolteacher. But his real passion is making documentaries about Turkey—he really loves the place. In the summer he drops everything for this, he'll take on any assignment he can get—travelogs, industrial films, commercials, short subjects, that sort of thing."

"And works all alone!" exclaimed Mrs. Pollifax.

Colin smiled wryly. "There's scarcely enough money in it for a crowd, but he does all right. As you can see, he picks up people like me when it pleases him, and then there are students in the summer, and in the winter there are mechanics and out-of-work seasonal people. It's all very casual but it functions."

"And your family like him?"

Colin wrinkled his nose. "Everything's relative, isn't it? He used to be *Sir* Hubert, with all the usual Ramsey accomplishments. Medals. Honors. Came out of World War Two loaded with that sort of thing, was knighted by the King and then one day took all the medals, flushed 'em down the toilet, packed a duffel bag and left England. A woman, my mother said. No, they don't *like* him but they leave him alone." He sighed. "It's hard to explain my family, they're not monsters, you know, they're marvelous really. Colorful, competitive, uninhibited, uncomplicated. I'd have absolutely no problems at all if—well, if—"

"If you were also colorful, competitive, uninhibited and uncomplicated," said Mrs. Pollifax, nodding.

"Yes." He grinned at her appreciatively. "But what brings you to Turkey?" he asked.

Mrs. Pollifax suddenly remembered why she was in Turkey and a sense of dismay chilled her. "The time!" she gasped, and looked at her watch only to discover that it had stopped. "Have you the correct time? I'm to meet a woman at eight o'clock in the lobby of my hotel."

Colin at once came to life. "I say—I'll take you back in the jeep! It's the least I can do after your bringing Mia's message, and it'll take my mind off my disasters." He glanced at his watch. "It's not quite seven—three minutes lacking. I wish there were more time, I could show you St. Sophia's on the way. Are you meeting your friend for dinner?"

"Friend?" Mrs. Pollifax was caught off guard. "Oh no— that is, I would like to take her to dinner but I don't know her. I mean, I don't know that she'll have the time for it. I'm only delivering—" She stopped, utterly appalled at the words she was letting slip. Really she must be more tired than she'd realized.

Colin Ramsey was smiling at her. "You know, you act just the way I do sometimes, but I can't think when or why. You stammered."

"I'm tired."

He shook his head. "No, you're nervous."

"Well, I shall be very nervous indeed if I'm late," she said, regaining control. "How long will it take us to reach the Itep?"

"The Itep!" he said. "Not the Hilton?"

Mrs. Pollifax suddenly and overwhelmingly realized why she was drawn to Colin, and she felt a small sense of alarm. They were alike. They had each lived quiet lives in the shadow of more dazzling personalities so that, somewhat submerged but no less intelligent, they had become observers. Acute observers. She recognized at once from Colin's question—so very akin to what she too would have noted— that he was weighing the Oteli Itep against what he saw and guessed of her, and the Itep did not fit, it introduced an unguessed facet of character that entertained and alerted him.

"The Itep, yes," she said firmly.

He looked amused. He arose and rinsed the two glasses under the faucet automatically, as if he were accustomed to looking after himself, probably over hot plates and wash basins in grubby London rooms, she guessed. "Ever ridden in a jeep before?" he asked as he led her across the courtyard.

"Never."

"All you have to do is hang on tight," he explained. "Hold your skirt down and your hat on." He glanced at her hat and smiled faintly. "It will be an experience for you."

"Yes," agreed Mrs. Pollifax, realizing that he believed he was giving her an event in an uneventful life.

"But I still hope you'll dine with me, which is what I was leading up to," he confided. "Blast it, I've eaten alone for three days now, and if you don't mind awfully, I'll wait and see what plans you make with your friend." He added wistfully, "I could show you both something of Istanbul, you know—it's beautiful at night. The Galata Bridge, the moon over the Golden Horn, and St. Sophia's at night is unbelievable. We could eat at Pierre Loti's, and—"

She felt the undercurrent of his eagerness: he was lonely. She said gently, "We'll see, shall we?"

"I'll park outside the hotel and wait until quarter past the hour," he said. "It's no hardship, you know, the streets of Istanbul are never boring." He shifted gears and they were off, sending up clouds of dust, and Mrs. Pollifax became too busy clinging to her hat to exchange further comments.

CHAPTER 5

IT WAS 7:35 WHEN MRS. POLLIFAX ENTERED THE lobby of the Oteli Itep, leaving Colin behind to look for a parking space and wait his alloted span of moments. She went upstairs, again washed her face in cold water, removed *Gone with the Wind* from her suitcase and locked her door behind her. Her mind was now functioning without blurredness; she was suddenly a courier, a secret agent, and she arranged the expression on her face accordingly. She realized that she ought to have taken the time earlier to explore the hotel—it would have been the professional thing to do—and so she walked upstairs instead of down—the hotel had no elevator—and discovered that the third floor was the top one. There was an interesting metal door to the roof: she tested it, looked out upon an expanse of flat tile, nodded approvingly and chose the narrow back stairs for her descent, virtually tiptoeing lest anyone point out that they were reserved for hotel personnel. The stairs ended in a shabby first floor landing with three exits: one into the lobby, one to the street, and the last to the basement. Pleased with her tour, Mrs. Pollifax walked into the lobby and sat down, book in hand, at precisely ten minutes before the hour.

It was a very Turkish lobby, its floor glowing with the colors and design of an unusually fine Turkish rug. The remainder of it was furnished with baroque statuary and old leather couches. Mrs. Pollifax had taken the couch near the back stairs, at some distance from the front, so that she was well out of the traffic between the main entrance and the larger staircase, and prominently displayed against the only window in the lobby. In fact she judged it to be the most conspicuous place possible, and she carefully arranged her book so that it was equally as conspicuous. With considerable suspense she watched the hands of the clock move slowly toward eight. The lobby was small, and there were only a few people waiting. Henry Miles had come in and was seated in a corner looking nearly invisible again, his eyes half-closed as if he were dozing. A young couple held hands in another corner and two men smoked and gossiped along the other wall.

It was when Henry glanced up that Mrs. Pollifax also looked to the entrance and became alert. It was precisely eight o'clock and a woman had entered the hotel. She brought with her a quality that changed the lobby so forcibly that Mrs. Pollifax wondered how people continued to walk and talk without awareness of it. What she brought with her—and to Mrs. Pollifax it pervaded the lobby—was fear. No, not fear but terror, amended Mrs. Pollifax: a primitive, palpable terror so real that it could almost be smelled and touched. The woman stood at the edge of the lobby, desperately trying not to be seen as her glance searched the room. Did her eyes ever so subtly drop to the gaudy book that Mrs. Pollifax held upright in her lap?

She cannot bear exposure, thought Mrs. Pollifax in astonishment; yet as she stood there, lacking the decisiveness to move, she was accomplishing exactly what she did not want: people were beginning to look at her. And certainly she was not a logical person to have entered a hotel lobby. Her dress was torn, old and shabby, the castoff plaid house dress of a European, and she was thin to the point of emaciation. But her face—what a beauty she must have been once, thought Mrs. Pollifax, seeing those deepset haunted dark eyes. Even her clothes, even the irresolution and exhaustion could not conceal the intelligence in those eyes. That head went up now, and the woman moved like a sleepwalker across the lobby until she came to Mrs. Pollifax. "Your book," she said in a low voice, only lightly accented. "You are—?"

"Sit down," Mrs. Pollifax said quickly. "You'll be less conspicuous and you do look exhausted."

The woman sank down beside her on the couch. "Who are you?"

"Emily Pollifax. Are you being followed?" Beyond the woman, on the other side of the window, Mrs. Pollifax saw Colin Ramsey sitting in his jeep. He had found his parking space and was patiently waiting for dinner companions. She felt that she had met and talked to him in another world, a world of innocence that had abruptly vanished at sight of this poor creature.

"I don't know, but—it is possible," whispered Ferenci-Sabo. "I should never have chosen this place—so far, so public, so open." She looked utterly wrung out, drained.

Mrs. Pollifax said crisply, "I've brought you money and a passport but obviously you need rest and food before you can use either. There's a rear exit on my left, do you see it? There are also stairs going up to the second floor. My room number is—" She broke off, startled. The woman beside her on the couch was staring across the lobby in horror. At once she jumped to her feet. "Oh please," she gasped.

Automatically Mrs. Pollifax glanced at the entrance to see what had frightened her; when her glance returned to the couch the woman was gone. She had vanished completely.

Two men in the uniform of the Turkish police were crossing the lobby, and one of them suddenly increased his pace, heading for the rear exit. His companion continued inexorably toward Mrs. Pollifax, and as he loomed above her—he looked surprisingly high—she doubtfully rose to meet him.

"Pasaport, luften," he said, holding out a hand.

"Passport?" faltered Mrs. Pollifax. "But what has happened? Do you speak English?"

"You are American? English?"

"American." She opened her purse, careful not to touch the second passport.

He opened and scanned the passport, glancing from face to photograph and back again. "You arrived here only this afternoon, I see." He frowned. "Your business in Istanbul?"

"Why—tourist," she faltered.

"The woman to whom you spoke—the one who fled—" He broke off as his comrade entered the lobby through the side door. His friend shook his head, pointed to the ceiling and disappeared again, presumably to search the hotel. Mrs. Pollifax's inquisitor nodded. "You will come with me please to headquarters, to Santral Odasi." His request lacked the courtesy of an invitation; his voice was authoritative, as was the hand he placed beneath Mrs. Pollifax's elbow. He had also retained her passport, which he placed now in his pocket. She had no recourse but to go. As they walked out, leaving by the side door, she was just in time to see Colin shift gears, maneuver out of his parking space and drive away, his profile without any expression except boredom, as if he had at last relinquished all hope of dinner companions. He did not even see her.

The officer behind the desk was in uniform; the second man, seated beyond him and introduced as Mr. Piskopos, was not. As Mrs. Pollifax seated herself she was aware that both men studied her coldly and clinically, as if to wrest from her who and what she was by psychic divination. She had the feeling that neither of them noticed her hat or her suit, or even the expression on her face, but looked beyond and inside, into motivation, into why her hands remained in her lap, why she gazed at them imperturbably and what she had to be concealing. Since at the moment she was concealing a great deal, Mrs. Pollifax practiced exorcising all memory of Carstairs and Alice Dexter White. She was an American tourist, she reminded herself, an American tourist . . .

"I am an American tourist," she said aloud in reply to the police officer.

Her passport lay open in front of him. He said dryly, "We have suddenly this week so many visitors to Istanbul. All tourists. This woman you were speaking to in the lobby of the Hotel Itep . . . you were there to meet her?"

"No," said Mrs. Pollifax calmly. "I was sitting in the lobby of the Hotel Itep resting before dinner."

"But you were speaking with this woman, were you not?"

"Oh yes."

"But you did not know the woman to whom you were speaking?"

Mrs. Pollifax said truthfully, "I had never seen her before in my life."

"That is not the point," said the police officer quietly. "Had you an arrangement to meet her, to speak to her?"

"She came up to me and asked for money," said Mrs. Pollifax firmly, "and I must say she looked as if she needed it."

"In what language did she accost you?"

"English," said Mrs. Pollifax, and suddenly realized the trap that had been set for her.

"English," he repeated politely. "In a Turkish hotel run by Turks, in the old section of Istanbul where few tourists lodge, a woman beggar comes up to you and speaks in English?"

"She must have guessed I was American," pointed out Mrs. Pollifax.

"Still, if she was only a beggar it is unusual that she could speak your language, is it not?"

Mrs. Pollifax sighed. "If you say so, but why is all this so important? Who is she?"

He looked faintly amused. He removed a square of cardboard from beneath his desk blotter and handed it across the desk to her, saying smoothly, "This is the woman to whom you were speaking." It was a question, yet stated so artfully that it was also a statement; he left it up to her to dispute or accept.

Looking at the snapshot he gave her Mrs. Pollifax saw that Mr. Carstairs and the New York *Times* might lack a photograph of Ferenci-Sabo, but that a very up-to-date one had begun circulating through Istanbul. It was certainly a picture of the woman she had met at the Itep, and a very recent one of her too. The eyes were half-closed, the face haggard and thin. Then Mrs. Pollifax noticed the dress Ferenci-Sabo was wearing, the same faded plaid, and she realized with astonishment that this snapshot had been taken of Ferenci-Sabo since she had reached Istanbul on Friday.

Had it been taken at the consulate? she wondered. In the confusion of the woman's arrival had someone really snapped her picture—or had it been taken of her *after* her abduction?

She looked at the police officer curiously. Was it possible that the Turkish government could have arranged Magda Ferenci-Sabo's abduction from the British consulate? For the first time she realized how important a defecting Communist agent must be to *them*. Russia was Turkey's next-door neighbor, their frontiers met and their guards faced each other for several hundred miles in the east. A great deal of practical information could be extracted from a knowledgeable Communist defector, and why should they share her when it was they who lived virtually under Russia's guns?

"Well?" demanded the police officer. "Is that the woman?"

"There's a resemblance certainly but beyond that—she left so suddenly! Who is she?" Mrs. Pollifax inquired again. When he ignored this she said quietly, "I really think I must refuse to answer your questions until I am told precisely why I am here, or am allowed to telephone someone who can inform me why I am here." She added severely, "I had understood Turkey was a country friendly to Americans—"

"To Americans, yes," the man said flatly.

She was surprised. "You don't believe that I'm American?"

The officer turned and exchanged a swift glance with the civilian behind him. "That is a possibility," he said.

"But my passport—"

He looked at her pityingly. "Passports can be forged." He hesitated and then leaned forward, frankly watching her face as he said with deliberation, "The woman to whom you were speaking is a woman wanted by the Turkish police, and one whom Officer Bey almost captured this evening. Her friends are of much interest to us—they may be our enemies. You arrived in Istanbul several hours ago, flying here directly without any tourist stops in between, and you meet this woman. A coincidence? We shall see." He touched her passport with a finger. "In the meantime—while we very thoroughly investigate your identity—we shall keep your passport."

She said indignantly, "I really must protest—"

He interrupted with a shrug. "You will, of course, notify your consul—we shall do this as well—but you are not to leave Istanbul, or the Hotel Itep, until you have been cleared to the satisfaction of all concerned." His expression lightened. "We should be able to return to you the passport by late tomorrow afternoon—if your credentials, how do you call it, check out. You may return now to your hotel, please." He did not shake hands; the other man, Mr. Piskopos, nodded curtly, and Mrs. Pollifax left.

In the police car, as it carried her back to her hotel, Mrs. Pollifax experienced something of the loneliness of the outcast. She had successfully met Ferenci-Sabo—this much was now obvious—only to see the woman frightened away; and now she had ignominiously lost her passport for twenty-four hours. What did she do next? What *could* she do? Did she go again tomorrow night to the lobby at the same hour? She could imagine Officer Bey's face should he see her there a second time at the same hour and clutching the same copy of *Gone with the Wind*. She did not concede failure as yet but she did admit to a deep discouragement and a certain amount of frustration.

She saw the hotel ahead, its exterior no longer nondescript at night under a blaze of neon color; somewhere along the pavement that other, nameless American agent had been pinned to a wall by an automobile. Mrs. Pollifax leaned forward. The taxi ahead of them slowed, turned, and pulled into the only empty space in front of the Itep to discharge Henry Miles—dear Henry, she thought fondly, and wondered what significance he had attached to her visit to police headquarters. His taxi drove away and as the police car in which she rode headed into the narrow opening another taxi suddenly cut in ahead of them, almost sideswiping them; a man leaped from it in a great hurry, pulled bills from his pockets, shoved them at the driver through the window and turned to run into the hotel. But something arrested him; he stopped, put his hands into his pockets and very casually sauntered across the pavement to the hotel. What he had seen, realized Mrs. Pollifax, was the back of Henry Miles disappearing into the lobby.

He was following Henry! thought Mrs. Pollifax in astonishment. It was no more than an impression but it was a vivid one: the haste, the panic, the fear of having lost sight of the subject, followed by the abrupt halt and even more abrupt change to casualness.

Only a few yards from here—somewhere beyond the front entrance, Carstairs had said—that other agent had been killed on Sunday night.

I can't let that happen to Henry—there must be some way to warn him, she thought in horror. Carstairs had said, *There may be a leak somewhere, or with so damn many agents in Istanbul they may be keeping one another under surveillance;* but what if Henry didn't know he had acquired a shadow?

She thanked her driver and walked into the hotel. There was no sign of Henry in the empty lobby. To the man at the desk she said, "There is an Englishman staying here, I saw him drop this earlier." She held up her small travel guide to Turkey and smiled at the man. "If you tell me his room number I should like to return it to him."

The translations took a few minutes and drew in the manager's son, who was fourteen and "took the English" in school, but had apparently not ventured beyond nouns and pronouns, and very few of those. A dictionary was produced and each word spelled out before it was understood what she wanted, and the boy offered to take the book himself to room 214.

"No, no—thank you," said Mrs. Pollifax, and then with another look at the dictionary added, "*Tesekkur edehim,* no."

She walked up the stairs, ignored her own door and continued down the hall. The door to room 214 stood ajar and the lights were on. She tapped lightly. When there was neither reply nor movement she tapped again and then swung the door wide and peered inside. "Henry?" she called in a low voice. She recognized his green suitcase on the bed, its contents scattered all over the coverlet as if it had been unpacked by the simple expedient of turning it upside down. Then she saw that every drawer in the tall chest along the wall had been left open, and his trenchcoat lay on the floor in shreds. She realized that while Henry had waited patiently for her outside the police station someone had been searching his room. But who? And where was Henry?

The curtains opening to the balcony trembled slightly, catching Mrs. Pollifax's eye, and her glance moved from the curtains to the open window and then to the darkness beyond. She shivered suddenly. *I'm not supposed to be here,* she thought. *I'm not even supposed to know Henry, and certainly I musn't be found here calling out his name.* His absence was alarming. Had he unlocked his door, switched on the light and retreated when he saw the state of his room? Was he even now down in the lobby complaining to the manager she had just left? Or had he stopped first in the public lavatory at the end of the hall?

She backed out of the room, touching nothing, and walked down the hall to the bathroom, but the door stood open and the room was empty. Mrs. Pollifax unlocked the door of her own room and flicked on the lights. Everything was in order, nothing had changed here except that a slip of white paper had been inserted under her door and glimmered white on the rug. "Henry!" she whispered in relief and picked it up, went to her window to check the lock, pulled the curtains and then unfolded the slip of paper.

But it was not from Henry, it was a message from the desk clerk on lined paper with the name of the hotel printed at the top. She read:

"9:02 Mr. Remsee fone. You lost pkge in his ownership. He bid you stop before—" The clerk had written *before tiring* but she judged the word was meant to be *retiring*. She read it a second time, frowning. What on earth did it mean? It seemed hours since she had seen Colin Ramsey, and with her mind on Henry it was difficult to think what package she could have left behind when she visited Colin that afternoon. She tried to remember what she'd carried with her to Ramsey Studios but aside from the signet ring, which belonged to Colin, there had been only her purse. Lost package! She'd lost nothing today.

Nothing except a defecting counteragent, she thought in horror, and forgetting Henry she snatched up her purse and fled the room, almost overturning several people on the stairs in her haste to reach the street and find a taxi.

CHAPTER 6

By NIGHT, ZIKZAK ALLEY LOOKED DESOLATE AND sinister, its buildings ghost-haunted. No light at all came from number twenty-three. A little worldlier now, however, Mrs. Pollifax walked down the narrow drive to the courtyard and was relieved to see thin stripes of light showing through the shutters of the kitchen window. She knocked on the door and it was opened at once by Colin. "What lost package?" demanded Mrs. Pollifax breathlessly.

Colin held the door wide and beckoned her in. "I say—I do hope they didn't give you a hard time!"

"Who?" she said, blinking at him.

"The police."

"You *saw*?" she flung at him accusingly. "You *knew* I was picked up by the police and you left? Just *left*?"

He was bolting the door behind him. "Of course," he said. "I was afraid you'd head for the jeep and talk to me. In that case the police would have headed for the jeep too, and would have noticed your friend—that woman who was sitting with you in the hotel window."

Mrs. Pollifax stared at him incredulously.

"I had her hidden in the back seat of the jeep, covered with a sheepskin," he explained calmly. "She was in a spot of trouble, wasn't she? Running out like that, looking like death itself—"

Appalled, Mrs. Pollifax stared at him. "You mean she was in your jeep when you drove *away*?"

41

He said patiently, "It's what I've been trying to tell you, yes. She came flying out, I leaned over and opened the door, said, 'Hop in—I'm Mrs. Pollifax's driver' or some such words. She fell in, I dropped the robe over her and that was that. A few seconds later the policeman followed and asked me if I'd seen a woman run from the hotel. I pointed out that I couldn't possibly see the entrance from where I was sitting without turning my head, but that no one had run up the street *past* me. Se he went the other way."

Mrs. Pollifax faltered, "But then—what did you do with her?"

He looked surprised. "Nothing at all—she's here. She's still in the jeep."

"Still in the jeep!"

"I couldn't rouse her so I simply locked the garage and left her there, and—what's the matter?"

Mrs. Pollifax had sat down very suddenly in the nearest chair. "You mean she's here? In that garage in back? In your jeep?"

Puzzled, Colin said, "Yes, of course. She *is* your friend, isn't she? I saw you together in the lobby and—"

Mrs. Pollifax began to laugh, she couldn't help herself. The laugh was a mixture of relief and hysteria but if it had a disquieting effect on Colin it was extremely therapeutic for her. As she wiped her eyes and blew her nose she said, "I simply can't thank you enough, Colin."

"Yes you can—you can tell me what the hell this is all about," he said, sitting down and looking at her sternly.

"About?" she echoed.

"That woman is no tourist. She needs blood transfusions at a hospital, not shish kabob at Pierre Loti's. What did the police want of you?"

"My passport," said Mrs. Pollifax sadly.

"Passport! You mean they took it away from you?"

"Yes, but only until they've investigated me."

He looked appalled. "But good heavens, you can't do anything without a passport—this isn't America, you know. You can't even change hotels without your passport!" He stared at her incredulously. "Doesn't the seriousness of this seep through to you at all? What on earth do the police think you've done? What reason did they give for taking your passport?"

Mrs. Pollifax sighed—she was beginning to feel very tired. "They seem to feel that I might have come to Istanbul to meet a notorious Communist agent."

His jaw dropped. "They *what*? *You*?"

"Yes," she said, and stood up. "Now I really must speak to my friend—speak to her at once—and then I'll remove her as soon as possible. I don't want to involve you—"

"Involve me?" he said angrily. "I'm already involved. What I'm trying to discover is what I'm involved *in*. You do know you're being followed, don't you?"

"You keep noticing things," she said with a sigh.

"Of course. I saw that chap walking up and down the alley when you were here this afternoon, but when I left you at the door of your hotel damned if he didn't follow you directly inside, and for all I know he's followed you here again, and is outside right now."

Mrs. Pollifax brightened. "Oh I do hope so," she said eagerly. "I tried to find him only half an hour ago at the hotel but I couldn't. That's Henry."

Colin looked taken aback. "Henry," he repeated blankly. "You know him then. Look here, who the devil are you? Or to put it more succinctly, *what* are you?"

She said sympathetically, "I'm Emily Pollifax, truly I am. I live in New Brunswick, New Jersey, and I'm an American citizen and I have two grown children and three grandchildren, and that's more than the Turkish police believe at this moment but it's absolutely true."

He put his hand to his head. "All right. Oddly enough I believe you, although I can't think of any *logical* reason why I do. But why did you come to Istanbul then?"

"To meet a notorious Communist agent," she told him cheerfully. "Now do please show me where the jeep is."

"You insist on being facetious," he told her bitterly. He removed a key from the shelf over the sink, opened the door for her and closed it behind them both. "This way," he said, and they walked in silence across the courtyard. A bright moon had turned the whitewashed buildings into ghost-silver and the bougainvillea threw jagged shadows over the cobbles. The sounds of the city were muted in this enclosure. Colin unlocked the door to the office and beckoned her inside. "She's in here," he said, and opened still another door and turned on the lights with a flick of his hand.

Mrs. Pollifax entered a double garage, at the moment containing only the jeep, a pile of abandoned tires and an orange crate. A shapeless bundle in the rear of the jeep stirred and lifted a head, shedding a sheepskin rug, and Magda Ferenci-Sabo blinked at the sudden light.

"Good evening," said Mrs. Pollifax amiably. "It seems that Mr. Ramsey has reunited us!"

Magda's glance moved from Mrs. Pollifax to Colin. "He is also—?"

Mrs. Pollifax sighed. "No, he is not," and for a moment both of them looked dubiously at Colin, who gazed stolidly back at them. "Colin," she said, "I wonder if you would mind—"

"No," he said crossly.

Mrs. Pollifax regarded him with interest. "You won't allow us a few minutes—?"

"No."

"What a difficult young man," said Magda.

Mrs. Pollifax smiled. "Yes, but he hid you from the police, this is his jeep you're occupying and this is his uncle's garage. Now we must think how to get you out of here. You *are* the woman I was sent to meet, aren't you?"

The woman looked at Colin. "It's better not to mention names, but there was a cable—"

Mrs. Pollifax nodded. "Yes, it was shown to me. Can you quote it?"

"I think so." Magda closed her eyes. "It read: Arrived six P.M., have enjoyed eight hours Öteli Itep, wish—" She opened her eyes. "If you were shown it perhaps you would be so kind as to complete it so that I too can be sure."

"Of course," said Mrs. Pollifax. "Wish you could join me why not send Red Queen or Black Jack before Friday."

"Look here," said Colin, regarding them uneasily.

"And the identity of Red Queen?" asked Mrs. Pollifax.

"I say," broke in Colin again, looking increasingly alarmed.

"Red Queen was Agatha Simms. I thought at first you

might be she but you're not. For my benefit—because you know so much about it—can you identify Black Jack?" asked Magda, and Mrs. Pollifax complied by bending over her and whispering the name of Carstairs. Magda nodded. "We understand each other—good. Now you must help me get to Yozgat, please."

Mrs. Pollifax looked at her blankly. "I beg your pardon?"

"Yozgat."

"Who on earth is Yozgat?"

Colin said testily, "It's a town, a Turkish town off beyond Ankara somewhere."

Mrs. Pollifax stared at Magda in astonishment. "But that's out of the question. I'm carrying a passport for you, all very legal and made out in the name of Alice Dexter White, and sufficient funds for you to get to America. You're to leave Turkey at once—and really you can, I think, in spite of all the furor because I've thought about it, and if I dye your hair and bring you some fashionable American clothes—"

A strangled gasp came from Colin but they paid it no attention. Magda sat up and said flatly, "I cannot leave this country yet, not even if it costs me my life."

"But you must," cried Mrs. Pollifax. "The police are looking for you—"

"I know, I know," admitted Magda, "and so are the Russians and the Bulgarians—"

An outright groan issued from Colin.

"—not to mention the people who kidnapped me from the British consulate and who are far more dangerous than any police." She edged her feet over the seat and dangled them. "But my life is of no significance at all if I leave without what I brought with me, and I *must* get to Yozgat. What is the trouble?" she asked of Colin, turning toward him. "Are you ill?"

He was sitting on the orange crate staring at them in open-mouthed horror. "My God," he gasped, "I'm harboring a bloody pair of spies! The two of you!"

"You insisted on listening," Mrs. Pollifax reminded him patiently.

"But she's that woman everybody's looking for!" He

looked haggard. "And she's sitting right here in my uncle's garage!"

"Yes, she is," admitted Mrs. Pollifax, "but really I'm trying very hard to think of where to take her, I *don't* want to involve you in this, you've already been so very kind—"

"Kind!" he said in a stricken voice. "Kind! You seemed like such a nice elderly lady!" He stopped, appalled. "I say, I'm terribly sorry, I didn't mean that the way it sounded." He looked even more appalled to discover himself apologizing. "Oh, hang it all," he said fiercely, and turning to Magda, "Do you know of somewhere to go?"

"Yes, to Yozgat," she said firmly.

"Magda—"

She turned to Mrs. Pollifax impatiently. "Why do you think they not kill me?" she demanded. "They want what I brought with me; I cross the Bulgarian frontier—do not ask me how—and I know I am followed so I separate myself from what I brought with me and I go instead to Istanbul for help. Now I must get to Yozgat, to recover what I bring. Do you not understand that—" She stopped uncertainly. "I hear someone."

"It must be Henry," said Mrs. Pollifax and turned toward the door expectantly.

But it was not Henry. Two square-shouldered bulky young men in trenchcoats stood in the door regarding them and the interior of the garage with interest. Magda caught her breath sharply. Mrs. Pollifax pulled herself together and said in a steady voice, "And who are you?"

The bulkier of the two men casually pulled a gun from his pocket.

"Police?" said Colin hopefully.

"I don't think so," Mrs. Pollifax told him regretfully.

Magda sighed. "Stefan and Otto, I grow tired with you. For what do you want to follow an old woman like me, hmm?"

Stefan grinned; it was a joke he appeared to appreciate and in such a stolid Slavic face his mirth was almost indecent. "We do not follow you—it is this one leads us here." He pointed at Mrs. Pollifax, who stared at him uncomprehendingly. "Who would have guessed the plump American partridge would know the wily Russian fox?" As he spoke his eyes continued to roam over the garage, mercilessly assessing the possibilities of the situation. Now he moved to Colin. "You will give the key to the jeep, please," he said, and extended his left hand, palm up, to Colin. Behind him his friend Otto also pulled out a gun.

"I say—it's not your jeep," Colin said indignantly. "It's not even mine, and you've absolutely no right—"

"The key," said Stefan, pressing the gun into Colin's stomach. "Otto, open the garage doors, and quickly."

Reluctantly, glaringly, Colin fumbled in his pocket and brought out a key that he placed in the palm of the man's hand. "You are wise," said Stefan. "Stay wise and you will live." Carefully he backed up until he reached the jeep, where Madame Ferenci-Sabo had begun making feeble attempts to climb out. With one arm he shoved her down. "Sit! Did you really think we wanted only a jeep?" he said mockingly. He opened the door and slid into the front seat, his head still turned to watch them. Only when the garage doors stood wide open did he insert the key into the ignition. Over his shoulder he called, "Don't forget our little souvenir, Otto!" To Mrs. Pollifax he said with a smile, "We do not wish to leave you emptyhanded. That would be quite unfair. We are like your pack rat, preferring always to leave something behind."

Mrs. Pollifax turned in alarm and looked toward the courtyard. From the shadow of the bougainvillea along the left wall Otto was dragging an inert and heavy bundle. She heard Colin, near the door, say, "Good God!" and she guessed by his whitened face that the burden Otto wrestled with was human. She watched in horror as Otto dragged a man into the garage; he placed the man at Mrs. Pollifax's feet and turned him over, and Mrs. Pollifax found herself staring into the vacant, unseeing eyes of Henry Miles. Dimly she heard Colin say, "You brutes," but his voice sounded miles away. She stared stupidly down at Henry, tears filling her eyes as she saw the small round bullet hole in his shirt. Henry had winked at her in the London air terminal, Henry had valiantly followed her since her arrival and now he was dead at her feet.

She looked up as the engine of the jeep roared into life; Stefan thrust the gears into reverse and she jumped back as

the car virtually catapulted from the garage carrying a
Magda who sat with eyes closed, her face unbelievably
white. The jeep neatly turned around in the courtyard, Otto
leaped in beside Magda, and the car shot up the driveway
and disappeared.

"At least the petrol tank's almost empty," Colin said in a
choked voice.

Mrs. Pollifax sank down beside Henry and looked into his
face. "He's dead," she said in a trembling voice, and placed
her hand over his heart but she could not change him. She
felt a million years old and deeply shocked. It had all happened so quickly. Four minutes earlier there had been only
the three of them here, talking about Yozgat. Now the jeep
was gone, Henry lay dead at her feet and Magda Ferenci-
Sabo had vanished a second time. Mrs. Pollifax looked
across the empty garage at Colin. He was standing in the
same spot, his mouth a little open in astonishment, his hand
still extended to give the man the key. He closed his mouth
now with a snap. "Do you know him?" he asked.

"It's Henry."

He nodded dumbly. "It was like a raid," he said, and then,
blinking, "They've taken your friend."

"Yes. And killed Henry." Neither of them were sensibly
communicating yet.

"And stolen my uncle's jeep." His lips thinned and he said
peevishly, "Damn it, I absolutely loathe being pushed
around." He walked to her side and leaned over Henry. "He's
really dead?"

"Yes."

"What are you going to do with him?"

It was an interesting question, delivered with the detachment born of shock, but it served to bring Mrs. Pollifax to
her senses, which had been badly jarred. "Why—I don't
know," she said in astonishment, and at once understood that
Henry dead could prove an almost insurmountable embarrassment, which was undoubtedly why Stefan had presented
him to them. "Good heavens!" she gasped, and stood up.

"We ought to have followed them," Colin said. "There's
still the van in the other garage but now it's too late. If they
go far they're bound to empty the tank, there was less than

five miles' worth left. We ought to have followed them. We can't keep Henry here," he added.

"No, we can't," said Mrs. Pollifax.

"Because you don't have a passport," he said, as if this explained everything.

She nodded. "I realize that. But I believe I know what to do with Henry. It's just struck me. I can take him to Dr. Belleaux."

"Who?"

"I was given the name of a man—a retired professor—to contact in an emergency."

"But with a *body*?"

Mrs. Pollifax thought about this. "I daresay it's unorthodox," she admitted, "but if he's equipped to handle emergencies can you think of any graver emergency than being presented with the body of a man who's been murdered? We have to consider your uncle, too; this is his garage."

"Yes," Colin said, nodding solemnly.

"Also," continued Mrs. Pollifax feverishly, "what else can we do with Henry? Stefan need only make one anonymous phone call to the police and I shall never get my passport back. And I have Dr. Belleaux's address right here in my purse. He's highly respected by the Turkish government—"

"Do you mean Dr. Guillaume Belleaux?" said Colin in surprise.

"Yes, do you know him?"

"I've heard of him. Everyone has."

"Well, I hadn't. But don't you see, he can vouch for me to the Turkish police! Of course we can't tell the police about Magda, but this time there's your jeep, with a registration number and a traceable license, and I can certainly describe to the police the two men who stole it. With this information the police may very well find both the jeep and the men by morning, and I shall have a clue as to where Magda may be!"

"Let's go then," Colin said, nodding. "The van's in the other garage. I'll back it up and we can put—uh—Henry inside." He disappeared through the door to the office and she heard an engine starting, garage doors open, and then a cumbersome van backed into the courtyard and Colin leaped out. "I think I'll turn the lights out for this," he said nervously and pulled the switch, leaving moonlight their only illumination. "You take his feet, will you? I'll take his shoulders."

Clumsily, slowly, they carried Henry to the van and inserted him into it. This proved extremely difficult because the van's rear doors had been welded closed—to gain more space inside, Colin explained breathlessly—and Henry had to be lifted up to the high cab of the van. Then it proved impossible to lift him between the two seats and they were forced to let him remain sprawled between the seats in a rather abandoned, drunken pose.

"I hope Henry doesn't mind," Mrs. Pollifax said breathlessly. "I mean his spirit, or whatever lingers behind."

"I suppose he's a spy, too," Colin said.

"Probably," said Mrs. Pollifax with a sigh, "although he was here only to keep an eye on me, to look after me, so to speak. Oh, if only I could have warned him!"

The van was moving ponderously up the driveway and now turned down Zikzak alley. "You said you have Dr. Belleaux's address?" asked Colin.

She disentangled it from the other papers in her purse and handed it to him. "The bottom one is the home address," she pointed out.

He glanced at it, memorized it and handed it back to her. "That's in the Taksim area. At this hour it won't take long. I know that street—very posh." He glanced down at Henry briefly. "Did you know him well?"

"No," said Mrs. Pollifax. "I was introduced to him in Washington just before I boarded the plane. But in London he winked at me, and he was one of the men who kept staring in fascination at my seat companion—why that was your sister," she recalled in surprise.

"He liked Mia," Colin said soberly, and Mrs. Pollifax realized that they were giving Henry the nearest thing to a wake possible.

They lapsed into silence, each of them involved in their own thoughts as the van negotiated the dark streets. Doubtless Colin was thinking of his uncle's jeep—another disaster for him, she mused—while she tried not to think of what might be happening to Magda, or what had already happened to Henry. It must have been his murder that she had interrupted when she entered his room at the Oteli Itep to warn him. She recalled the curtains fluttering at the balcony window and shivered: his body must have lain behind those curtains. It was rather obvious now that Stefan had also hidden behind those curtains, and heard her call to Henry—and then she had led the murderers straight to Magda. *I should never have gone to Henry's room,* she thought sadly. *Mr. Carstairs warned me—no, ordered me—to have no contact with him at all. How could I have forgotten? One soft-hearted moment and I betray Magda.*

And Magda, she remembered, had been her assignment. Not Henry. In retrospect all kinds of ingenious little ideas came to her: she could have sent the manager's son to room 214 carrying the guide book as well as a note for Henry, whom she had believed to be alive then. Or she could have slipped an anonymous warning under his door and fled. But no, she had gone instead to his room and entered, calling out his name, and now his enemies knew that Emily Pollifax, too, was not what she appeared to be.

They were passing over the Galata Bridge now, and the lights of moving tugs and boats slashed the glistening inky water with long ribbons of gold. Even at midnight the bridge was filled with traffic: mules, trucks and donkeys bearing fruits and vegetables to the markets and merchandise to the bazaars. Pale moonlight etched out the silhouette of the mosque at the foot of the bridge and touched each passerby with a high light of silver. Mrs. Pollifax sighed and forced herself back to the moment, and to arranging explanations for the Dr. Belleaux whom she would presently meet. "How is it that you've heard of Dr. Belleaux?" she asked Colin. "Is he really that well-known?"

"To live in Istanbul is to hear of him," he said. "The police consult him on murders—he writes and lectures about criminology, you know—and the archaeologists consult him on bones, that sort of thing. He's quite lionized as an author and scholar. Goes to all the 'in' parties."

"What does he look like?"

"My impression is that he's fiftyish, or early sixtyish, with a pointed white goatee. Rather thin, talkative, elegant."

"I do hope he's of a practical nature."

"You mean practical enough to dispose of a body?" commented Colin dryly. "Ah, here's the street, I told you it was an impressive one."

"Indeed yes," she said, looking out upon well-spaced villas surrounded by charming gardens. The homes on the street were dark except for one in the center of the block that blazed with light. It was at this house that Colin applied the brakes. "You're in luck," he said. "Dr. Belleaux is not only up but from the look of all the cars parked here he's giving a party as well—and they've not left much space to get through, damn it." He leaned out and swore, maneuvered the van through the line of cars, turned around and came back, cutting the ignition and the lights. "Here we are," he said. "What do you plan to do?"

"I'd not expected a party," she said. "I shall have to ask to speak privately to Dr. Belleaux. I think I shall tell them at the door I'm from the American embassy—is there one?"

"They're all consulates here."

"All right, then I'm from the American consulate. That will do until I can get Dr. Belleaux aside and explain myself and *try* to explain Henry."

"Would you rather I pull into the drive?" he asked. "A bit awkward unloading in the front."

"Later—I want to be able to find you again," Mrs. Pollifax confessed. "This may take a little time. Would you care to come too?" She was growing rather attached to Colin, she realized.

"I don't feel I should leave Henry, do you? If anyone walked past and happened to glance in—"

His voice trailed off as a car rattled up the avenue, sputtering and backfiring, to turn into Dr. Belleaux's driveway a few feet away from them. At the crest of the drive the car shuddered to a halt, a man jumped from the rear seat and gave it a push—it was a jeep—and then leaped in as the car coasted down the driveway to the rear.

Mrs. Pollifax drew in her breath sharply. "Colin," she said incredulously. "Colin—"

"I saw it," he said in a stunned voice.

"I'm not losing my mind?"

"No," he said, and then, quickly and incoherently, "Damn it, no. Even the petrol—I told you the tank was almost empty and you saw him pushing it. Damn it, that was my jeep!"

"But here?" whispered Mrs. Pollifax. *"Here?"*

"It was Otto—I swear it—who jumped out and gave it a push," he said. "And that must have been your friend slumped in the back. Are you coming?" he demanded. He opened the door and jumped to the pavement.

"I certainly am," she said fervently. She could not imagine what kind of mix-up she had stumbled into. There had to be some reasonable explanation, but it would have to be delivered to her at a more appropriate moment. Stefan and Otto simply *couldn't* be working for Carstairs, too; not when Magda had virtually identified the two of them as her abductors. And they had killed Henry. But why were they *here*?

"Just a minute," said Colin, and reached into the compartment of the van to extract two lethal-looking guns. "Don't expect them to fire, they're made of wood," he whispered. "They're props Uncle Hu made for a short subject on Ataturk."

"But I'm delighted he did," she told him.

Props in hand they hurried down the driveway, moving from shadow to shadow until they came to the corner of the house. But already it was too late. Mrs. Pollifax had hoped they might arrive in the rear to find the jeep's motor still running, Stefan and Otto off guard and Magda still accessible but the jeep had been abandoned. The back door to the house stood wide open, the screen door still swinging gently, but although a great deal of light and noise came from the building there were no humans to be seen.

"Damn," said Colin. He looked intently at Mrs. Pollifax. "You're not going to knock and ask for Dr. Belleaux." He might have intended it as a question but it came out as a flat statement.

"No."

"Are you going to call the police?"

She said gently, "From what you've told me of Dr. Belleaux a number of the police are probably inside at his party. And I don't have a passport. No—I'm going to risk a look inside."

He looked shaken. "I say, that's rather dangerous."

She said steadily, "Perhaps it will be but I really don't

know what else to do. As you may have guessed, I came to Istanbul only to meet and help Magda—and she's in there, and I'm responsible."

He nodded. "Then I'm going in with you."

She looked at him. "Colin, I can't let you become any more involved, I really can't. I have to remind you that all I did was deliver a message from your sister this afternoon—"

"Yesterday afternoon by now—"

"—and you'd never seen me before in your life. This is going to be very illicit, I may get caught, and you've said yourself that you're a physical coward."

He said fiercely, "Of course I'm a coward but I absolutely loathe being pushed around—I told you that—and these men stole my uncle's jeep, dumped a dead man in our garage and kidnapped your friend. Now do let's stop talking—of course I'm going with you!"

Mrs. Pollifax smiled faintly. "All right," and returned her glance to the house. It was a two-storied rectangle of pale stucco with blue shutters. She wondered if Stefan and Otto had gone upstairs or down to the basement but there were no clues. She tiptoed to the screen door and peered inside; directly opposite, scarcely five feet away, a back staircase rose steeply toward the top of the house. Her decision had been made for her: they would try the upstairs first. "Look," she whispered, pointing.

To the right lay a long kitchen, brightly lit but empty of people although she could hear the sound of running water from a distant corner. Mrs. Pollifax slowly opened the screen door, testing for squeaks. Nothing happened and she slipped inside and across to the staircase with Colin directly behind her. She did not pause until she was halfway up the stairs. Here the rising sounds of the party proved an irritant: it was a very large party and the murmur of voices rose and fell in waves, but if they concealed any sounds that she and Colin made they had the disadvantage of concealing approaching footsteps as well. She felt trapped in noises all of them confusing; still, she could not remain exposed on this stairway for any length of time and so she rallied, brought out her absurd wooden pistol and moved to the top of the stairs.

Here she met a wide carpeted hallway containing six

doors, all of them closed. On her right, at the far end, the hall terminated in a stairwell and the carpet overflowed the stairs like a waterfall of gold; it was from this end of the house that music and conversation rose almost deafeningly. Mrs. Pollifax headed in the opposite direction, on the supposition that these rooms were farthest removed from people, and people would be what Stefan and Otto must avoid if they were here, and the thought of their being here—of all places!—still baffled and shocked Mrs. Pollifax.

The first door they opened was a bedroom but except for ornate hangings and baroque furniture it was empty. The second door proved to be a linen closet. With some impatience Mrs. Pollifax threw open the door to the third room, only to be reminded that impatience bred carelessness, for this time she had opened the door to a bedroom containing three people—the impact took her breath away—and in unison, also stunned, three people turned to stare at her.

It was as if she had abruptly cut the switch on an unwinding reel of film. Magda lay across a chaise lounge like a bundle that had been flung there, and Stefan, leaning over her, looked up in the act of withdrawing a hypodermic needle from her arm. Otto stood on guard a few feet from Mrs. Pollifax, his mouth open as he stared at her. He was the first to react: he moved so swiftly, so menacingly, that without a second to think about it Mrs. Pollifax lifted her right hand, flattened it as Lorvale had taught her, and dealt Otto a crisp karate chop to the side of his throat. He stared at her in astonishment and then his eyes closed and he sank slowly to the floor. Behind her Colin gasped, *"Mrs. Pollifax!"*

"Get his gun," said Mrs. Pollifax crisply.

Colin stooped and plucked it from the floor, pocketing his own wooden prop. Holding the live gun he gestured Stefan away from Magda. "Against the wall," he ordered, waving the gun with growing enthusiasm.

Mrs. Pollifax, her flowered hat only a little askew, went at once to Magda, who was trying to stand. "Can you walk?"

"I'm drugged," she said in an anguished voice. "Hurry!"

Mrs. Pollifax nodded, and, grasping her arm, led her to the door. Colin followed, walking backward with his gun pointed at Stefan. But Stefan refused to remain abjectly against the wall: he took one step and then another, following Colin with a nasty grin on his face.

"There's no lock on this door!" Colin said desperately, trying to slam it in Stefan's face.

Mrs. Pollifax glanced back over her shoulder. Magda had already begun to sag and it was doubtful that she would remain upright if Mrs. Pollifax withdrew her arm to help Colin. Obviously Stefan was determined to follow them; he knew the gun was loaded because it was Otto's, but he was not going to make it easy for Colin, who was so patently an amateur. To hesitate for long would risk their having to literally carry Magda out of the house in their arms. "If he comes too close, shoot him," she said calmly, and headed down the hall to the stairs.

But at the top of the rear staircase Mrs. Pollifax stopped in dismay, for the downstairs hall and entrance that had been deserted ten minutes ago was now aswarm with workers. The screen door through which they had entered was propped wide open. Buckets of ice were being carried in and empty trays wheeled out to a waiting truck. A heavy-set butler stood at the bottom of the stairs calling out orders and completely blocking the exit. He did not look as if he would give ground easily, or let them through unchallenged.

Mrs. Pollifax turned away. They had to get out of the house quickly, before Magda lost consciousness, and there was no alternative now but to use the main staircase. Propping up Magda she half-carried her to the stairwell, grasped the banister and began a step-by-step descent. They made a ludicrous procession, she thought, herself and Magda clinging together in the vanguard, followed by Colin walking backward and brandishing a pistol at Stefan, who continued to leer and follow three paces behind. As they descended Mrs. Pollifax could look down and see the massive oak door at the foot of the stairs. She knew that beyond, parked in the street, stood Colin's van; if they could just get through that door . . .

The piano playing came to a sudden halt. Slowly the murmur of voices subsided into startled silence and Mrs. Pollifax found herself in full view of Dr. Belleaux's party; she was in fact staring down into dozens of gaping faces. She supposed that two women on the stairs might have gone unnoticed but that the sight of Colin holding a gun made for a certain conspicuousness. Rather wearily—it had been a long and violent evening—Mrs. Pollifax lifted her wooden gun and addressed the sea of faces below her. In her most imperious voice she said, "I will shoot the first person who tries to stop us." It was a phrase culled from the late late movies but it was the best that she could manage under the circumstances.

Someone said, "Get Dr. Belleaux!"

Mrs. Pollifax reached the bottom of the stairs and pulled open the door, holding it wide. As Colin backed into her, stepping painfully on her ankle, she said in a low voice, "Take Magda and run."

He nodded and pressed the functioning gun into her hand. "Thanks—I couldn't possibly shoot it," he admitted.

"I can," she said calmly. "Just get her out, she's going under."

It was now Colin who bore the sagging Magda into the night and down the path, and Mrs. Pollifax who faced Stefan. "I am going to shoot the first person who walks through this door after I leave," she called out, only a little embarrassed by her clichés. To her left, from a corner of her eye, she saw several people move apart, and for just one moment she allowed her glance to leave Stefan: she looked into the livingroom and into the eyes of the party's host who had suddenly appeared. She thought, *Dr. Belleaux, I presume*, and then her glance swerved back to Stefan, she saw him coiled to jump at her and she fired the gun at the ceiling above him. Slamming the door behind her, she ran.

Colin was bundling Magda into the van across the street but unfortunately Henry was already there, which had led to difficulties. When Mrs. Pollifax reached the van Colin was starting up the engine with a dead Henry at his elbow and an unconscious Magda in the passenger seat. "Jump in somewhere—anywhere," he cried in a harassed voice. "Try the floor or sit on Henry. Or Magda."

Mrs. Pollifax climbed in and fell across Magda just as the van began to move and a second before it raced down the street. "I'm heading for the ferry, I'm going to get you out of Istanbul right now, before all hell breaks loose," he said, and he turned on the van's lights as they reached the corner. "You can't go back to your hotel, and the first place Stefan will look for you is Ramsey Enterprises, and after that they'll begin watching the ferries and the airport. There's not a minute to lose; the ferries don't run as often at night."

"I'm a wanted citizen," Mrs. Pollifax said in a surprised voice.

Colin looked at her and grinned. "Well, look at the facts, Mrs. Pollifax," he suggested. "The police have your passport and will be looking for you, Stefan and Otto will be looking for you, you'll be wanted for burglarizing—not to mention kidnapping—and have you noticed the interesting passengers we've acquired? At the moment I can't think how to explain a dead man with a hole in his chest or a woman who's been heavily drugged."

Mrs. Pollifax looked at him. "Colin," she said accusingly, "you *enjoyed* it!"

"Good God, it was terrifying," he said. "What I am experiencing is the absolute relief at still being alive. Who would ever have believed we would get away with it! I say," he added, "shouldn't you do something about Henry before we reach the ferry?"

Mrs. Pollifax agreed; and as the van careened through the empty streets she alternately tugged and pulled Henry into the darkest shadows of the van.

CHAPTER 7

AT THE KABATAS LANDING STAGE THEY ENCOUN-
tered their first stroke of luck: a ferry was being
readied to leave its slip. Ropes and chains were
being cast off, but the gates had not yet closed. With a flour-
ish Colin drove the van onto the ferry; only one more car
followed and the gates swung shut. "But there are telephones?" pointed out Mrs. Pollifax bleakly.

"There are telephones, yes. Keep your fingers crossed
that no one will be waiting for us on the other side!"

As they crossed the Bosporus they undertook a frenzied
and certainly bizarre housecleaning of the van's rear, which
had been casually equipped for living purposes. Under
Colin's tutelage they set up a battered old army cot and
chained it to the wall, placed a still heavily drugged Magda
on it and covered her with blanket. They rolled Henry under
the one piece of built-in furniture in the van: a high work-
bench which Colin explained was used for developing
photographs, cooking meals on a sterno and even, in emergencies, as a bed. "Do you think the people at Dr. Belleaux's
party saw the van clearly enough to describe it?" asked Mrs.
Pollifax, covering Henry with a blanket, too.

"From the window anyone could have seen the shape of
it," Colin said. "But the license or its color, no. It was too
dark—the nearest light was far down the street. But you
know they need only inquire what vehicles belong to Ramsey Enterprises to learn the registry number and description.

There's the jeep, and this van, and then the second van that Uncle Hu's taken to Erzurum. Do you think Stefan overheard Magda insisting on going to Yozgat?"

Mrs. Pollifax said in a dismal voice, "Probably." She sighed. "It does seem the most wretched luck that Magda's drugged again and can't explain more. My orders were to get her out of Turkey quickly—to save her life at any cost—and I don't *like* this Yozgat business. I've finally found her, and it would still be relatively simple to put her on a plane, whereas Yozgat—" Her voice trailed off uncertainly and she shook her head. "I don't even know where it is yet!"

"I don't mind dropping you off there," Colin said. "I've thought about it, you know. I can't go back to Istanbul until this blows over and I've decided to keep going and find Uncle Hu. He's the only person who can untangle all this—for me at least—and he should be starting back from Erzurum tomorrow morning."

"Colin—"

He smiled. "I know, I know, you hate to see me involved. It's purest chivalry, of course—I'm cursed with it. I was raised on King Arthur."

"I think that's rather charming," said Mrs. Pollifax thoughtfully, "but you're taking me on face value alone which alarms me."

"Rum, isn't it?" he said smiling, and shrugged. "I can't possibly explain it—call it a hunch or an instinct. Or put it this way: How can I possibly drop all this now and never know how it turns out? Good God, the thought appalls me. And do you realize that tonight—for the first time in my life—I've been involved in something I actually pulled off successfully? It's positively dazzling. In the meantime your friend Magda seems to attract the most unwholesome bunch of toughs I've ever seen, and I can't say very much for your other friend—I mean Dr. Belleaux, of course."

"I can't say very much for him, either," said Mrs. Pollifax with feeling. "I think that Mr. Carstairs would be extremely surprised by what we've seen tonight, too."

"Who?"

"Mr. Carstairs is the gentleman who—uh—arranged my coming here."

Colin said with a crooked smile, "To have sent you he

must have a real sense of humor. There's the warning bell—come along to the front of the van, we're almost there."

"Oh," said Mrs. Pollifax in a hollow voice, turned off the flashlight and crept back into the passenger seat.

The ferry nudged its way into the slip, chains rattled, gates opened and engines warmed up. The cars ahead began to move, and Colin inched the van forward. Slowly they drove off the ferry and into the night: no police whistles shrilled, no one ran toward them shouting at them to halt. They had crossed the Bosporus and left the peninsula of Istanbul behind without incident. "Now where are we?" inquired Mrs. Pollifax and brought out her guide book.

"No need for that," said Colin. "This is Uskudar, formerly Chrysopolis, and noted mainly as a suburb and for its enormous Buyuk Mezaristan, or cemetery."

"Cemetery!" exclaimed Mrs. Pollifax thoughtfully.

Colin looked at her. "You can't possibly—"

"But we must find somewhere appropriate to leave Henry." He groaned. "You look so extremely respectable, you know."

"I have a flexible mind—I believe it's one of the advantages of growing old," she explained. "I find youth quite rigid at times. Why *not* a cemetery?"

Colin sighed. "I daresay there's a certain logic there. You're not—uh—thinking of burying him as well?"

"That would be illegal," she told him reproachfully, "and scarcely kind to Henry."

"Sorry," he said. He peered out at a sign, and nodded. "This is the avenue—I think we're driving alongside the cemetery now. Watch for an entrance, will you?"

Several moments later they left the world of trams, lights and occasional automobiles and entered a subterranean night world of awesome silence. "This is the cemetery?" faltered Mrs. Pollifax.

"It's a cypress grove, quite huge. There's a sultan buried in the old part. I'd call the new part spooky enough."

"But what curious headstones!"

"They're Moslem, of course. The steles with knobs on the top represent women, the ones with turbans are men. Then there are variations—I've forgotten them—for priests and those who've gone to Mecca."

The van bumped to a jarring halt and he cut the motor. At

once the silence was filled with an overwhelming drone of chirping grasshoppers and shrilling cicadas; the volume was incredible, as if they had entered a jungle. The headlights picked out tangles of sinister dark undergrowth and the silhouette of hundreds of headstones leaning in every conceivable direction. The moon, dimmer now and trailing clouds behind it, sailed over the forsaken scene and added a ghostly pallor to the tombs. When an owl hooted mournfully Mrs. Pollifax jumped.

"Well," said Colin, and flicked off the headlights.

"I suppose you had to turn off the lights?" said Mrs. Pollifax as both darkness and insect noises moved in on them.

"I really don't think we're supposed to be here," Colin pointed out reasonably.

"I can't think why not," she said bravely, and climbed down from her seat.

Clumsily, laboriously, they carried Henry from his hiding place and lifted him down to the damp grass. "Where do you want him?" asked Colin.

Mrs. Pollifax ignored the irony in his voice. "Over by that larger stone, I think. We want him to be noticed soon but not immediately. Do you think those horrid men took his identification?"

"Probably," gasped Colin as they carried Henry across a path that felt like a brook bed, up a small slope and to the larger, paler headstone that had caught Mrs. Pollifax's eye. "Don't show a light!" he said sharply.

"I'm writing his name and the name of his hotel on a slip of paper," she explained. "There! Henry Miles, care of Oteli Itep." She leaned over and tucked it into the pocket of his dark jacket. "I should like someone to do as much for me," she said firmly. She stood a moment looking into the eerie black shapes of gnarled tree trunks, creeping shrubbery and mooncast shadows. "He was a very nice man," she said at last. "Now, do let's leave."

"What did you do—roll 'im?" said a deep, lazy, amused voice from the darkness.

Mrs. Pollifax turned and saw a shadow detach itself from the darkness of the tomb. A giant of a man arose, stretched himself calmly, yawned and strolled nonchalantly toward them. In the dim light he looked seven feet tall but this was a trick of shadows—Colin turned on the flashlight, and he shrank to a more reasonable six feet. His face was swarthy, with dirty scraggly hair and a stubble of a beard. He wore filthy sailors' pants, a jacket that had once been white, a frayed turtle-neck sweater. His feet were shod in a pair of old sneakers with a hole in each toe.

Colin said bravely, "Who the devil are you, and what are you doing behind that gravestone?"

"Sleeping," said the man, looking down at them. "Til you drove in and woke me up." He put his hands on his hips and surveyed Mrs. Pollifax with interest, his eyes moving appreciatively over the flowered hat, lingering on her face, then smiling as they took in the navy blue suit, white blouse and shoes. He shook his head. "Now I seen everything!" He dropped to the ground and peered at Henry. "He's dead," he said. "You shoot him?"

"No."

"Then what the hell."

"Someone else shot him," Colin said crossly.

"We didn't know what else to do with him," explained Mrs. Pollifax. "Since we just happened to be passing by— why are you here?" she asked sternly.

"That's my business." He stood up and looked at them. "A couple of tourists dropping off a guy with a bullet hole in his chest!" He shook his head. "Now wouldn't the police like to hear about that?"

Mrs. Pollifax stiffened. "Nonsense. I very much doubt that you can afford to talk to the police."

He laughed; his guffaw threatened to awaken even the dead. "You got a suspicious mind. Okay, so I'm sleeping in a graveyard. So I'm broke. So you got a corpse, it makes us even. You also got a truck and you're gonna drive it out of here. I need to get out of here. I had it in mind we might make a deal." His voice caressed the last word. "Wotthehell, how about it? I'll take a lift if you're going in the right direction."

"Which direction is that?" asked Colin cautiously.

Cunningly the man replied, "Which direction you heading?"

Mrs. Pollifax realized that she wasn't certain of this herself. "How *do* we proceed?" she asked.

"Toward Ankara."

"Perfect!" said their new companion, beaming at them. "Got a friend there that owes me money."

"Have you a passport?"

"Of a sort."

"What's your name?"

"Sandor's enough. Just Sandor."

"Greek?"

"Of a sort."

"A sailor?"

The man was clearly laughing at them now. "Of a sort."

"Can you drive?" asked Mrs. Pollifax.

"I can drive."

Mrs. Pollifax exchanged glances with Colin. "An unholy alliance," commented Colin.

"Sheerest blackmail, of course," said Mrs. Pollifax cheerfully.

"But mutual," pointed out Colin with a faint smile. "All right, Sandor, we'll give you a lift."

"Of course," he said. "But on a condition."

Mrs. Pollifax stiffened. "Oh?"

"No monkey business—no stops. I don't want no welcoming committees in Ankara."

Mrs. Pollifax smiled. "That—uh—fits our plans quite well," she conceded graciously. "You know a way to Ankara that avoids—uh—welcoming committees?"

"Know the city like the back of my hand!"

"A veritable jewel," she murmured.

As they walked back to the van Colin said in a low voice, "Of course you realize he's wanted by the police."

"Then he's in good company," she pointed out in a kind voice. "What would you guess his crime to be?"

"Smuggling's big along the coast, and if he's been a sailor he's probably been involved in smuggling. Opium, probably."

"Opium," repeated Mrs. Pollifax, and smiled. "So now we have joined the underworld! How very surprising life can be . . . !"

CHAPTER 8

THEY DROVE ALONG NIBBLING AT THE GRAPES WITH which Sandor had equipped himself for his night in the graveyard. Following his initial shock at discovering they already had a passenger—"She dead, too?" he had asked with professional interest—Sandor announced that he was going to sleep before he did any driving. "But I'll know if you stop," he said, drawing a serviceable gun from a pocket. "I'll sleep on the floor. Any monkey tricks and I'll shoot."

"Why didn't you show your gun earlier?" asked Mrs. Pollifax curiously.

His glance was withering; obviously he felt that his wits and his tongue were sufficient for gullible foreigners. "Did I need to?" he asked with a shrug. "Now, drive." Whereupon he lay down on the floor of the van, curled up and began snoring.

The moon that had perversely haunted them hours earlier now disappeared just when it would have been the most appreciated, and to further depress Mrs. Pollifax the road to Izmit was bumpy. At first the Bay of Kadiköy cheered her with its cluster of lights, and later there were sustaining glimpses of the Sea of Marmora but presently a light rain began to fall, blurring all the lights and with it any hope of sightseeing. Mrs. Pollifax's thoughts darkened equally: she had neither slept nor eaten anything of substance since her arrival in Istanbul and she was beginning to feel the lack of

65

both: lemonade and grapes served only as an appetizer for a dinner that moved increasingly out of reach. She was also beginning to feel the irregularity of her situation: having never in her life received so much as a parking ticket she was under suspicion by the police in this supposedly friendly country, and presently she might even become the subject of a nationwide alarm. She had arrived in this country with Henry, and Henry was dead. There was no one at all to whom she could appeal—certainly not to Dr. Belleaux now—and her companions in exile were a young British misfit and a disreputable blackmailer acquired in a cemetery.

It was difficult to figure out just how it had all happened. *Perhaps I'm too flexible,* she thought, and turned to scrutinize Colin beside her. She was not a fool. There were high stakes involved in this assignment, and many crosscurrents which she would probably never know about. It had already occurred to her that Mia Ramsey could have been artfully placed on the plane beside her to girlishly suggest looking up Colin. But there had been no certainty that Mrs. Pollifax would contact Colin at all, and several hours later it was Colin who had saved Magda by concealing her from the police. If he were part of a vast and sinister scheme it was doubtful that he would have telephoned and left a message asking Mrs. Pollifax to retrieve her lost friend; Magda would instead have disappeared forever. No, she had to regard Colin as a small miracle.

The van's headlights picked out pretty little suburban villas and strange place names: Kiziltoprak, Goztepe, Caddebostani Erenkoy, Saudiye, Bostanci. At a town called Maltepe the road met the sea again and followed it on to the seaside port of Kartal. To keep Colin awake Mrs. Pollifax read the road directions from the small guide book she had purchased in London. When this palled she read from the same book brief histories of the Ottoman and then the Seljuk Empires until a listless Colin complained that Sandor's snoring was more stimulating than ancient history. They then argued whether, once past Izmit, they should drive to Ankara by way of Bolu or Beyzapari.

"Which is the route people usually prefer?" she asked.

"Bolu. The road's excellent."

"Then I think we should go by way of Beyzapari."

They were still arguing this when they reached Izmit at half-past three in the morning. As they crossed the railroad tracks to leave the town they saw the first brightening of the horizon in the east, and seeing it Colin nodded. "All right, Beyzapari. The thought of getting to Ankara quickly is very tempting—after all, it's 292 miles and we've gone only sixty—but if dawn's coming, and the police will be looking for the van, then I concede we might not get to Ankara at all if we go by Bolu. By the way, what exactly do you expect— being an experienced undercover agent," he added dryly.

"I am not an undercover agent," said Mrs. Pollifax tartly. "I'm a courier. As to what I expect I would say just about anything, but that's because of Dr. Belleaux, you see."

Colin said wryly, "You've not yet found that rational explanation for Magda's being carried off to *his* house?"

"No I haven't," she said frankly, "and the really frightening part of it all is that he's a man whom everyone trusts. Carstairs told me he enjoys the confidence of the Turkish and American governments and you've described him as being a consultant to the police here and enjoying *everyone's* confidence. I seriously doubt that Carstairs would even remotely consider Dr. Belleaux's being involved in any treachery."

Colin said dryly, "Which leaves us the only two people who think otherwise? Damn it, that's a horrible thought!"

"Yes it is," said Mrs. Pollifax, and shivered. "But no matter how kind we try to be to Dr. Belleaux there's no getting around the fact that while he gives parties in his downstairs livingroom there are two chaps upstairs drugging a defenseless woman."

"Definitely a double standard there," agreed Colin.

She nodded. "His reputation makes it so patently unfair! There's no way to fight him—except to run, and I'm not sure that running is sensible, either, since it leaves him with an absolutely free hand. Just think of the possibilities open to him!"

"It's better you don't," Colin said gently.

Mrs. Pollifax nodded. He was quite right: they would be rendered helpless, like the tiger in a tiger hunt, with the police and Dr. Belleaux—separately or even together—beating the bushes in a steadily diminishing circle until they were isolated and then flushed out. "At least I have Magda," she said, but since she did not have the slightest idea of what to do with Magda, or how to get her safely out of the country before the police found them, this was not essentially comforting.

"Could you get word to your friend in Washington?" Colin asked.

"I don't know," she said slowly. "I was given strict orders not to. I was also given strict orders never to contact Henry; but then I did, you see, in order to warn him he was being followed, and you know what a monstrous mistake that was. I led Stefan straight back to Magda. A cable to Mr. Carstairs might do the same thing. Do you need to show a passport to send a cable?"

"Probably. I have mine with me but of course by the time we get to Ankara the police may very well be looking for me, too."

"Yes," said Mrs. Pollifax in a depressed voice, and resumed staring out of the window.

Beyond Izmit the road dipped down to Geyve and then wound up again through hills covered with fields of wheat and tobacco. Dawn found them on a high plateau beyond Goynuk, and then they reached a pass and coasted down into a plain. Beyond the town of Nallihan Colin suddenly pulled the van off to one side of the road and braked to a stop. "We've gone nearly a hundred and sixty miles and I'm tired," he said, mopping his forehead with his sleeve. "Sandor's going to have to pay his way now. Sandor," he called. "It's morning—half-past seven—and your turn to drive."

"What the hell," said Sandor, making a great deal of noise yawning. "This lady back here is staring at me," he complained. "Is there breakfast?"

"There's a camp stove somewhere," said Colin, "and the water jug is full, I filled it myself—Uncle Hu is always very fussy about that. And I believe there are bouillon cubes, dusty but soluble."

"But that's wonderful," said Mrs. Pollifax with feeling. She crawled back to Magda who was staring at the roof of the van with a puzzled expression. Seeing Mrs. Pollifax she said in a weak voice that bore a trace of irony, "Where am I now?"

"It's a little difficult to explain."

"Who was that man who snores so dreadfully?"

"That's even more difficult to explain. How are you feeling?"

"Weak and very thirsty. I have been drugged again?"

Mrs. Pollifax nodded. "It might be wise for you to get some fresh air now. It's very hot back here. Colin is making broth for you."

"Colin! That funny young man is still here?"

"The situation is extremely fluid and unconventional," Mrs. Pollifax told her, "but we *are* moving in the direction of Yozgat." She helped her to her feet, and out of the van to the roadside where Colin had set up his sterno.

Colin was saying, "Presently we'll be crossing the Anatolian plain and there will be even more sun, wind and dust." The water he was nursing came to a boil, he stirred bouillon into it and carefully divided it among four battered tin mugs. "Here you are," he said.

Never had Mrs. Pollifax tasted anything kinder to her palate: at first she rolled the broth on her tongue, savoring its wetness, and then she drank it greedily. "Purest nectar," she said with a sigh, and saw that color was coming back into Magda's white face for the first time. "At what hour do you think we will reach Ankara?" she asked.

Sandor was noisily smacking his lips. "With me driving we go like the wind. Another forty miles to Beyzapari, beyond that sixty maybe." He was studying the van. "She has a Land Rover body?"

Colin nodded. "She's a rebuilt Land Rover, yes. Four-wheel drive and all that."

Sandor nodded. "Very good! By early afternoon we get there, or near enough. Then we go by back roads. They are very bad," he added regretfully, "but very very private."

"You are wanted by the police?" inquired Mrs. Pollifax companionably.

Sandor grinned. "You are a nice lady but you ask too many questions. In Ankara I have fine friends and I let you go free."

"Free?" said Mrs. Pollifax with amusement. "I didn't realize we'd been captured."

He patted his pocket with meaning. "I have you under guard, beware. Now wotthehell, let's go."

For some moments Mrs. Pollifax had been aware of a small piper cub plane drifting lazily along the horizon at a distance; she had watched it as Sandor talked. Now with one foot on the running board of the van she said in an alarmed voice, "Colin, look!" For the plane, having momentarily disappeared behind a ridge ahead of them, had suddenly reappeared now and was flying toward them at a shockingly low altitude. Colin stood behind her carrying the camp stove and squinting at the sky. The sound of the plane's engine grew frighteningly loud and for a moment Mrs. Pollifax wondered if they were going to be strafed: the plane passed so low that she could clearly see the face of the pilot, who in turn looked down at them; and then just as abruptly the plane's nose lifted, it climbed and began a long circle that carried it over the ridge again and away toward Ankara.

"Damn fool," Sandor shouted, shaking a fist at the horizon.

Colin said in a choked voice, "What the devil does that mean!"

"Reconnaissance, I think," said Mrs. Pollifax. "But by whom?" She was rather unnerved by the incident; until now she had felt safely removed from Istanbul, but she resolutely put aside her anxiety, helped Magda back to her cot and insisted that Colin have the dubious honor of napping on the floor because he was the more tired from driving. Again she took the passenger seat, this time beside Sandor, and they set off—or rather flew off, thought Mrs. Pollifax, clinging to the sides of the leather seat, for Sandor drove with abandon, swerving gaily around the holes in the road, swearing in Turkish and English at the holes he did not miss, and frequently taking both hands off the wheel to rub dust from his eyes or to light an evil-smelling cigar which almost immediately was extinguished.

They climbed now to a ravined and arid plateau, and the dust they raised all but obscured the sun. It was hot, the van captured and retained both the heat and the dust, and their water supply was gone. Since leaving Nallihan they had passed only one car and that one had been abandoned beside the road—probably with a broken axle, thought Mrs. Pollifax ominously. Nothing moved except the mountains on the horizon, which swam in the rising heat like mirages, until far ahead of them Mrs. Pollifax saw an approaching cloud of dust. "Dust storm?" she inquired—it was impossible to doze at all with Sandor at the wheel, and he had just finished telling her that dust storms were frequent in summer on the road to Ankara.

"Car," he said briefly.

Mrs. Pollifax nodded; she had begun to feel that if Sandor said it was a car it would be a car—and as it drew nearer it was indeed a car, a very old dusty touring car of 1920 vintage. The sun shone across its windshield, turning it opaque, so that as it approached them it appeared to be driven by remote control. It was therefore all the more startling to Mrs. Pollifax when she saw a hand and then an arm extend full-length from the passenger side of the car. When she saw the gun in that hand she stiffened. "Watch out—a gun!" she cried, and ducked her head just as the windshield in front of her splintered.

Sandor virtually stood on the brakes. "Wotthehell," he shouted, and fought the steering wheel to get them off the road.

Behind her Colin shouted, "Stay down, Mrs. Pollifax!"

Metal protested, tires squealed and Mrs. Pollifax's hat fell off as the van lurched across the ridge that contained the road; they bumped uncomfortably over untilled ground. Sandor was tugging at his belt with one hand; he brought out his gun but the car had already passed them: the sound of a second bullet rang *ping!* against the rear of the van.

In alarm Mrs. Pollifax turned and saw that Colin was reacting with astonishing efficiency; he had remembered that he had a gun, too, and now he was slashing at the glass in the round porthole window in the back; as she watched she saw him lift the gun he had taken from Stefan and push it through the window. She thought he fired it, but there was too much confusion to know. Sandor was swearing as he fought the wheel again, turning the van to head it back to the road.

"Look out!" screamed Mrs. Pollifax as the van swung around, for the ancient dust-ridden car had also turned and was heading toward them at accelerated speed, hoping to ram them if it couldn't shoot their tires first. For a second the van's wheels spun uselessly in a gully, then Sandor roared the engine and the van shot back on to the road just as the elderly Packard left it. A bullet zoomed over Sandor's head, again just missed Mrs. Pollifax and went out the open window. But Sandor had fired, too. He seemed to have three hands, one for the gearshift, one for the wheel, and one for firing. With a wrench of the wheel he turned and backed the van and tried to shoot down the car but the Packard swerved, circled and returned to the road to face them head-on.

They remained like this for several seconds, each car facing the other on the road with a distance of perhaps twenty yards between them, each driver revving his engine and waiting. Then with a burst of noise the Packard started down the road at full speed, heading directly toward them. *"Hoooooweeeeee,"* shouted Sandor, his eyes shining—it was clearly a game to him—and he recklessly steered the van straight at the Packard, not giving an inch. Mrs. Pollifax screamed and slid from seat to floor. From here she looked up to see a familiar face—Otto's—almost at their window, saw the Packard hurtle past them, barely missing them. As the Packard passed from sight she heard Colin's gun begin firing from the rear window, heard the scream of tires, a terrifying sound of metal twisting and turning, twisting and rolling, and Mrs. Pollifax put her hands to her face. "They've turned over," cried Sandor, braking, and leaped out.

Mrs. Pollifax slid from her side of the van and jumped to the road. The Packard was lying upside down in the dust after rolling over several times. Mrs. Pollifax began to run. "We must help them," she cried, and then suddenly the silence was rent by a great explosion and flames turned the Packard into a funeral pyre. Mrs. Pollifax stepped back and covered her eyes. "Did anyone get out?" she gasped in horror.

Colin was beside her with a hand on her shoulder. He looked pale and shaken. "No," he said. "I watched. It was Otto driving, and a man I'd never seen before doing the shooting."

Sandor said belligerently, "What the hell goes on here, they maniacs? Nuts? They tried to kill us!" He looked incredulous. "What the hell they want?" he said, shaking a fist.

"Us," Mrs. Pollifax told him in a trembling voice.

He gaped at her. "Those jerks were gunning for *you?*"

Mrs. Pollifax nodded a little wearily. "Yes. First they sent the plane—there must have been radio communication, and then—"

Sandor looked from her to Colin and back again. "But why?" he demanded indignantly.

Mrs. Pollifax said weakly, "They apparently didn't want us to get to Ankara."

"That I could see for myself but what the hell's going on?"

Mrs. Pollifax hesitated and then recklessly took the plunge. "You might as well know, Sandor, that not only *those* men are after us but the police, too."

"Police!" He stared blankly. "You?"

"Yes."

His mouth dropped. "You *did* shoot the guy you was unloading in the cemetery!"

"No," she said patiently, "but Otto did—the man driving the Packard."

A light of comprehension dawned in Sandor's eyes. "I'll be damned," he said, and to Mrs. Pollifax's surprise he gave her a look of grudging admiration. "I'll be damned," he said again, scratching his head, and then he began to laugh. "You're crooks too!" he cried delightedly.

Colin interrupted primly. "I say, I resent that very much!"

Sandor was wiping his eyes with a filthy handkerchief. "No offense, I know we're not in the same league." He grinned at them both. "So when I picked you up in the cemetery back there—and you let me come along like that—you was really picking me up!" He shook his head admiringly. "I thought I had you two scared to death of me."

Mrs. Pollifax said soberly, "I don't think we should stand here talking like this. I think we should leave before someone sees the smoke and comes to find out what's happened. Colin, do go back and reassure Magda." Still she remained standing and staring at the smoldering wreckage. "It could have been us," she said with a shudder. "They intended it to be us. Sandor, you did a remarkable job of driving."

He was still regarding her with amazement. "That guy Colin had a gun—he had it all the time. And you got gangsters after you—I picked a helluva bunch of people to hitch a ride with!" The expression in his eyes was one of infinite respect. "I know a guy could use you. You want to make some real money? I'll introduce you when we get to Ankara."

"I'm not sure Ankara's a good place for us to head," said Mrs. Pollifax sadly. "Not now. There may be roadblocks. And thank you but I don't need any 'real money,' I just want to get safely out of Turkey."

Sandor nodded wisely. "That bad then," he said, escorting her back to the van. After handing her up to the front he appeared to have reached a decision. "You come to Ankara," he said firmly. "Ankara's the place for you. I got good friends there, you hear? A little crooked"—he shrugged and grinned—"but wotthehell, you need help. If anybody can smuggle you into Ankara it's me, Sandor, and there my friends help you, wait and see."

Mrs. Pollifax looked into his face and was touched by his concern. "Thank you, Sandor," she said simply.

From the rear of the van Colin said bitterly, "He probably thinks he's bringing his pals two bona fide members of the Mafia."

CHAPTER 9

IN LANGLEY, VIRGINIA, IT WAS TUESDAY MORNING, just half-past eight and already over ninety degrees in the streets. Carstairs had arrived in his air-conditioned office high in the CIA building and was sipping a second cup of coffee as he read over dispatches that had come in during the night. He had just lighted a cigarette when Bishop walked in. "Sir," he said.

"Yes, Bishop, what is it?"

He held out a sheet of paper. "It's a routine report that arrived at the clearing office a few minutes ago from the State Department. They shipped it up here as fast as they could. It seems that during the night the State Department received an urgent request from Istanbul for the verification of one Mrs. Emily Pollifax, an alleged American traveling under an allegedly American passport."

"What the devil!" said Carstairs, scowling. He took the sheet of paper and stared at it. It was, as Bishop had said, one of the routine memos that circulated through a number of channels until it ended, heaven only knew where, as a fifth copy of what already had been filed in the Passport Division of the State Department. Its message was innocent enough but reading it Carstairs experienced his first uneasiness.

"I don't like it," he said.

"No, sir."

"I don't like it at all."

"No, sir."

"I see it's stamped five-fifteen A.M. upon arrival here. What time would that have been in Istanbul?"

"Nine-fifteen last night, sir."

Carstairs swore. "Only an hour following Mrs. Pollifax's first attempt to meet Ferenci-Sabo then." He didn't understand, of all the people moving in and out of Istanbul, what on earth could have drawn the attention of the police to Mrs. Pollifax? Her passport had been arranged on a top-priority basis and had been processed in less than an hour; had there been something important omitted in the processing? Had it appeared different or even forged to the police? No, that was impossible, he had double-checked it thoroughly himself.

"This is not calculated to induce calm," he said dryly. "When the police single out one person out of thousands—and that person happens to be an agent of ours—then a certain bleak note enters the picture." He shook his head. "We can't contact the Istanbul police, our interest would only produce a reaction that would be the despair of our diplomats—the right hand must never know what the left hand is doing," he added, and stubbed out one cigarette and lighted another.

But a possibility had occurred to him. "We can't do anything directly, Bishop, but we can be devious. Contact Barnes over in the State Department. Ask him if he'd mind cabling our consulate over there in Istanbul, in his name, to ask why the hell the Turkish police questioned the legal passport of one of our American citizens. I've got a meeting upstairs in five minutes but keep me posted if it lasts longer than I expect."

"Yes, sir. He's to make his inquiry routine but ask for immediate information?"

"Right. If the police have gone so far as to question Mrs. Pollifax the consulate ought to know about it. If they don't know, they'd jolly well better find out. I'm curious to say the least!"

"Right, sir."

When Carstairs returned from his meeting there was still no word. He sat back and reflected upon Mrs. Pollifax's schedule. She would have arrived in Istanbul about four yesterday afternoon—at least he knew now that she had arrived safely, he thought dryly. But at nine o'clock, or soon after, the Istanbul police had sent off a cable asking that her credentials be verified by the American government. Routine curiosity? Was the Hotel Itep under surveillance now? Had Mrs. Pollifax been injured, or even killed?

The reply, when it came in from the American consulate, was brief. The Istanbul police had questioned one Mrs. Emily Pollifax for half an hour during the preceding evening but they refused to say why they had taken her to central headquarters for questioning. They had retained her passport for twenty-four hours; upon receiving verification of her identity they were now prepared to return the passport to her. Mrs. Pollifax had not been located yet, however. She was registered at the Hotel Itep but had not been seen there since late Monday evening.

At this Carstairs swore again, briefly but savagely. "Not been seen! Not been located! And she doesn't have her passport?"

"No, sir," said Bishop. "They're still holding it for her."

"Thank God she's got Henry with her, but where the hell can she go without a passport?" demanded Carstairs. "Damn it, I'm helpless. I can't find out one blessed thing without endangering Ferenci-Sabo as well as Mrs. Pollifax, not to mention the goodwill of the Turkish government."

"There's Dr. Belleaux, sir."

He shook his head. "Not yet. I wanted absolute secrecy on Mrs. Pollifax—and I've got it, blast it, in fact I'm stuck with it. I'd contact Henry before I risked anyone else—but if Mrs. Pollifax is not in the hotel then it's not likely he'd be, either. Bishop, someone's knocking on the door."

"Yes, sir." Bishop opened it and returned bearing an inter-service message. "From Barnes, sir, in the State Department. He's heard from the American consulate in Istanbul again."

"Again?"

"Yes, sir. He's scrawled a note here saying he doesn't know what's up—or want to—and he's too much of a coward to phone you with this news."

"What news?" asked Carstairs in a hollow voice. "Read it, Bishop."

"Yes, sir. It's a cable: REGRET INFORM YOU BODY OF AMERICAN CITIZEN HENRY MILES—"

"*Body?*" echoed Carstairs in a stricken voice.

"Yes, sir. Shall I go on?"

Carstairs nodded, his face grim.

"—OF HENRY MILES DISCOVERED EARLY THIS MORNING IN USKUDAR CEMETERY STOP."

"Cemetery!"

"ONLY CLUE HANDWRITTEN NOTE APPENDED TO BODY QUOTE THIS IS HENRY MILES HOTEL ITEP STOP POLICE HAVE IDENTIFIED HANDWRITING AS BELONGING TO—" Bishop suddenly stopped and swallowed hard.

"They've got a lead?" broke in Carstairs savagely. "Get on with it, Bishop, for heaven's sake!"

—"BELONGING TO MRS. EMILY POLLIFAX, AMERICAN CITIZEN OF—"

"What?" exploded Carstairs.

—"OF NEW BRUNSWICK, NEW JERSEY, AND REGISTERED AT SAME HOTEL."

"Oh no," groaned Carstairs.

Bishop nodded. "Yes, sir. Emily is cutting quite a swath, isn't she? There's one more sentence, sir—"

"Then finish it," growled Carstairs.

"WARRANT ISSUED FOR HER ARREST."

"Good God," said Carstairs and slumped back into his chair. "Henry dead—our second agent killed inside of forty-eight hours over there; Mrs. Pollifax missing, and not a single word on Ferenci-Sabo." He sighed and shook his head. "It just about ends our attempt to contact Ferenci-Sabo, Bishop. If Mrs. Pollifax is still alive—and there's no certainty that they didn't get her, too—she's been rendered helpless without a passport. What can she do, where can she go? We'll have to proceed on the assumption that she can be of no more help to us."

"Yes, sir."

Carstairs rubbed his brow. "But we've still got to keep that lobby covered every evening until Friday—just in case. Is Hawkins still in London?"

Bishop nodded.

Carstairs sighed. "Apparently it's like dropping people into a bottomless well to send them to Istanbul, but we must keep trying. Fix up a telephone connection, will you Bishop? I'll give Hawkins the most superficial of briefings and if Ferenci-Sabo is still alive—the chances grow less every hour—he'll have to hide her in a cellar somewhere until we can think what to do next. Damn," he added.

"And Mrs. Pollifax, sir?"

Carstairs nodded. "I was coming to that. Send off a cable to Dr. Belleaux, Bishop. Alert him to the fact that Mrs. Emily Pollifax is one of our people, and may try to reach him, in which case we'd appreciate his giving her what help he can without bringing the roof down upon all our heads."

"Yes, sir."

Again he shook his head. "Not much else we can do for her, Bishop." He added irritably, "Oh, and add a full description of her for Dr. Belleaux so that he'll know precisely what she looks like, Bishop—and don't forget that damned flowered hat!"

CHAPTER 10

CAREFULLY SANDOR INCHED THE VAN THROUGH streets so narrow the houses could be touched on either side. Frequently their passage was halted by a donkey ambling ahead of them, or by women carrying jugs of water on their heads. There was no coolness in the shade. It was three o'clock in the afternoon and sun and dust lay heavy in the alleys, trapping smells of spices, charcoal, olive oil and manure. Mrs. Pollifax's impression of their entry into Ankara had been chaotic: they appeared to have approached the city by means of a dried-up river bed over which they had clattered and bumped, half-circling Ankara before darting furtively across one tree-lined boulevard to vanish into the old town. As they climbed higher now in this maze of streets Mrs. Pollifax glimpsed the top of the citadel ahead and then lost it. A moment later the van halted; Sandor wrestled furiously with the steering wheel and backed the van slowly, laboriously, through a hole in a crumbling wall. Bricks toppled and a fresh cloud of dust enveloped them.

They emerged in a courtyard, abandoned except for a solitary goat, tied to a ring in the wall, who lifted his head and brayed at them in protest. An old adobe building opened into the courtyard, its roof open to the sky, its walls giving shade to the few sparse tufts of grass on which the animal fed.

Sandor cut the engine. "We walk now but you wait first," he said firmly. "I go find Bengziz Madrali. He is receiver of stolen goods—I make sure he receive *you* now."

"How long will you be gone?" asked Mrs. Pollifax anxiously.

He shrugged. "I have to find him first, then I know how long I'll be gone. If anyone comes, hide in the old *khan*." He was gone before Mrs. Pollifax could protest.

"What's a *khan*?" she asked Colin.

"An inn." Staring at the gate through which Sandor had vanished he said, "I rather like him but I can't think why."

"That's very reassuring since we're completely dependent on him for the moment," Mrs. Pollifax pointed out. "Do you like Magda too?"

His gaze left the gate to sweep the courtyard. "She seems pleasant enough when she's not drugged. But then she nearly always is, isn't she?" He brightened. "I say, that looks like a Hittite frieze propping up that door. Hand me my camera, will you?" He began to prowl through the litter around the door, keeping a respectful distance from the goat, who watched him with suspicion.

"How nice to see you again!" Magda said cheerfully, crawling from the interior of the van to sit down beside Mrs. Pollifax on the top step. "Perhaps you can tell me where we are?"

"We've reached Ankara." She noted that Colin had disappeared with his camera into the ruins of the *khan* and she turned to Magda urgently. "We've not been able to talk and you must realize that from my point of view this journey to Yozgat is on faith alone. What *is* it that we go to Yozgat for?"

Magda hesitated. "I dare not say, not yet at least. But let me tell you this: I go to Yozgat to find the people who smuggled me out of Bulgaria and into Turkey." She was thoughtful for a moment and then she added quietly, "I do not know how you feel about gypsies. People hate and fear them. Perhaps you are not aware that in spite of—or because of—people's revulsion towards gypsies they were able to do a number of valuable things for the Allies during World War Two—those who were not wiped out by Hitler."

"Gypsies!" exclaimed Mrs. Pollifax in surprise.

"Yes. Some are nomadic and wander all over Europe while some have settled down, like the gypsies in Istanbul who live in what is called the Tin Village." She said almost shyly, "It is with them I hid when I first escaped Stefan and Otto and waited for you."

Mrs. Pollifax said in astonishment, "Do you mean it's the gypsies who got you across the border into Turkey?"

She nodded. "To be accepted by them is not easy, the Rom look on *gorgios* with deep contempt. But many years ago we worked together, I gained their trust, I learned their language, I know a few of them as true friends, and to know a few is to be accepted by them all. Yes, it was with them I crossed the border and it is to the Inglescus that I entrusted everything when I realized I was being followed. They promised to wait for me at Yozgat for a few days before they continued south to their rendezvous, a wedding later in the summer."

"But this is remarkable," said Mrs. Pollifax, delighted. "You have your own private underground!"

Magda's smile deepened. "You put it well. But please, you will remember the name Inglescu if anything goes wrong with me? Find them and say Magda sent you. They will understand."

"But can they be trusted with what you left them?"

"Yes," she said flatly.

"I can't help wondering why you suddenly left your old life. You understand that I was told the whole story about you. Did they find this out?"

Magda smiled. "No, they discovered nothing. I decided to retire."

"Retire!" cried Mrs. Pollifax.

"Yes, retire." At the expression on Mrs. Pollifax's face she burst out laughing. "But did you never think of people like me wishing to retire? I will no doubt be a shock to them— agents are not supposed to survive as long as I, they are supposed to die violently and early. But me, I have just gone on surviving—such an embarrassment!—and without even paying dues to the Social Security."

"What will you plan to do?" asked Mrs. Pollifax eagerly.

Magda shrugged. "I bring my own social security with me, as you will see. I have no plans except I wish to live a quiet life now, I want to plant flowers and watch them grow, feel sun on my face, think good thoughts, have real friends. I am tired of violence, of uncertainty and betrayals, of remaining always detached lest someone I grow to like must be betrayed, or betray me. Most, I am tired of acting the double part. This is how it began, I was an actress on the stage in Vienna, but who would guess I play the roles so long, day and night, on and on."

Mrs. Pollifax looked at her and was curiously touched. She thought of the *Times* biography which could not know or possibly describe—no one could—the complications or dangers which this woman must have met and mastered with intelligence and courage, and always alone. But she thought the story was written clearly in the lines of Magda's face: *Those are good lines,* she thought, *lines of humor and compassion and deep sadness. And I heard her laugh—how did she escape corruption from all this?* Her hand went out to touch Magda's hand and squeeze it. "There is one thing," she said quietly. "Something that complicates our getting to Yozgat and to the gypsies."

"Yes?"

"Before I left Washington I was given the name of a man in Istanbul to whom we could appeal for help if we needed it. A very reliable person whose name is Dr. Guillaume Belleaux."

"Yes?" said Magda with interest. "But that is reassuring."

Mrs. Pollifax shook her head. "The house in which you were drugged last night—the house to which Stefan and Otto took you—turned out to be the home of Dr. Guillaume Belleaux."

Magda's lips formed an O and her eyes widened. "*Mon dieu* but that is *not* reassuring! So this man is—but is he aware that you know this? Did he see you?"

"Yes to both questions." Mrs. Pollifax shook her head wryly as she recalled her exit from Dr. Belleaux's house and the face briefly glimpsed across the livingroom. "He may not have seen Colin, no, but he and I looked at each other across the room. Briefly but memorably."

"Then he is the one behind all this—he too plays the double game!" Magda reached out and gently touched Mrs. Pollifax. "It is a lonely business, this, is it not? I'm sorry. My God I'm sorry. But we must stay alive a little longer to annoy him, yes?"

"Yes," said Mrs. Pollifax but she winced a little as she reflected upon the odds: they did not speak Turkish and they were moving deeper and deeper into Turkey's interior; the police, Stefan and of course Dr. Belleaux were looking for them. She did not even know if Sandor would return, and without him they would be almost completely helpless. She thought that he would come back but he was, after all, a man of doubtful character. Still, it was his temperament, not his character, that was in their favor: she was trusting to his curiosity and to his Machiavellian nature to bring him back, if only to arrange what would happen next.

She looked up and waved at Colin who had wandered out of the inn. He said dreamily, "Just think, these same walls were standing when Tamerlane came through this part of the country." He patted his camera. "I think I got a wonderful shot of that frieze, and the old walls inside; I'm absolutely certain I didn't muff it. No Sandor yet?"

"Here he comes," said Magda.

Mrs. Pollifax looked up to see him loping through the gateway and she had to control her gladness at seeing this disreputable, grinning, filthy man. She thought that even if he shaved and bathed she would recognize him because he would still exude the same boundless joy in living and in outwitting whatever forces resisted him. He had obviously been busy for his arms were full of bundles.

"I am back," he cried. "I have found Bengziz Madrali and he will help—there is much work to do, we go to meet him now but first—good Turkish peasant clothes so you will become incognito."

"Become what?" said Mrs. Pollifax, staring with distaste at what appeared to be a week's laundry that he held out to her.

Obviously he was conferring a great honor upon her. "For you ladies the baggy pants," he said. "Also the skirt, the shirt and the shawl that begins over your heads and goes everywhere—I show you its workings." He stuffed them into her arms without sympathy. "And for you," he cried happily to Colin, "the moustachio—a good sweep of one—and a cap and trousers with holes in them. You will look like me, eh? Could anything be better?"

"Oh nothing," Colin said dryly.

"Then wotthehell, change now in the truck and we go. Is better Madrali never see you in your own clothes, he has a feel for intrigue, that man, and the roadblocks are up."

Mrs. Pollifax had been halfway across the courtyard with her new clothes in her arms when he said this. She stopped. "Roadblocks?"

He nodded pleasantly. "Twenty minutes ago. *Pfut—*

suddenly they are there. Police stopping everyone. Madrali hears everything, you understand? He says officially it is the new government study of traffic flow but he hears they look for specific peoples." Sandor beamed at them. "You do not wish to be specific peoples, do you? Incognito please—at once!"

Mrs. Pollifax thought the room looked exactly like a thieves' den, and she discovered with some surprise that she felt delightfully at ease in such an atmosphere. Shadows leaped up the walls and across the ceiling from candles burning in their sockets and from the charcoal brazier on which their dinner of *tel kadayif* and *pilaf* had been cooked. On one whitewashed wall hung a picture of Ataturk in an unusually convivial, smiling pose. On the other side of the brazier, seated cross-legged on the floor with a tray on his lap, Bengziz Madrali squinted over the three cards of identity he was forging for them. Occasionally he grunted expressively as he examined his work through a jeweler's glass, and occasionally he flashed Mrs. Pollifax a smile laden with warm reassurance and admiration.

"Your name is now Yurgadil Aziz," commented Sandor, eating noisily with his fingers from a platter and looking over Madrali's shoulder. "The other lady is Nimet Aziz, and he"—pointing a dripping finger at Colin—"is Nazmi Aziz."

Lost: one Emily Pollifax, she thought, and glanced ruefully at the black baggy pants engulfing her legs.

From the corner Magda gave an amused laugh. Her hair had been dyed brown from a bottle that Madrali had purchased in the bazaar; and then it had been washed and set in fat steel curlers that bristled gruesomely all over her head. She sat and smoked a Turkish cigarette with elegant fastidiousness, her hands moving gracefully but without any sign of being attached to her body, which had become lost somewhere inside her voluminous Turkish disguise. Near her sat Colin, loading his still camera with film for the passport photograph he was going to take of Magda when the curlers were removed and her hair combed. Catching Mrs. Pollifax's glance he said irritably, "Soon? You know I've got to develop the picture and then it's got to dry!"

In appearance she thought he outdid them all. He wore shabby pinstripe trousers tied with a belt of rope, a vest too tight across his chest, a purple shirt and a pink bowtie. His sweeping moustache left him almost mouthless and because he wasn't accustomed to it he kept trying to look down at it, which caused his eyes to cross. He also complained that it itched. Yet in spite of all this he had acquired a definite air of distinction. In some indescribable manner his new identity brought out the fierceness in him that Mrs. Pollifax had noticed when she first met him but which she had assumed was a defense against failure, and against taller and more successful men. But freed of any possible competitiveness, and wearing the most absurdly shabby clothes, Colin *was* fierce. There was no mistaking it: there was a look about him of a mountain brigand.

There is more of his family in him than he knows, thought Mrs. Pollifax with amusement. She stood up and walked over to Magda and felt her head. It was dry. Removing the curlers she said, "Mr. Madrali, you have the suntan make-up? You have the white backdrop for the passport picture?"

"Evet, evet," he said, nodding. "Over there, pliss."

Colin shook his head. "I still can't imagine how you expect to get her out of the country when we can't even get out of Ankara."

"I go look into that now and make more questions," Sandor said, reluctantly putting aside his plate of food. "The new ideas they come and go. Now I go."

"Good. The white blouse, please," said Mrs. Pollifax, helping Magda out of her Turkish clothes and into her own navy blue suit.

Sandor stopped and looked down at Magda. "Wotthehell she can't leave a country without a passport."

"She has a passport," Mrs. Pollifax said calmly as she began applying tan make-up to Magda's white face.

"Wotthehell, you forge those too?"

"It's a very respectable passport," she told him, "and very legal. There," she said, applying lipstick to Magda. "I think she looks rather like a poetess or an undernourished actress, don't you, Colin?"

Sandor went out, looking mystified. Colin said, "You're quite right, I wouldn't have believed it possible."

Flashbulbs illuminated the room several times before its native dimness returned, and then Magda lay down and promptly went to sleep. Colin at once became tiresomely cross and nervous about developing the film, and since Mr. Madrali's English was severely limited and he was still engrossed in his forgeries, Mrs. Pollifax opened the door and walked out.

The tiny house in which Mr. Madrali lived—or hid, as the case might be—leaned against the walls of the Citadel, even belonged to the wall of the Citadel, like something washed up against the sides of an old ship. Mounting the tamped down earthern path behind his house Mrs. Pollifax put back her head and looked up at the wall that had withstood a thousand years of earthquakes, pillage and armies, and then she looked down at the crooked, meandering alleys below, with their rows of primitive hovels dropping to the base of the hill. The sun was just disappearing behind the distant mountains leaving a blaze of glorious color in the sky but on the plains surrounding Ankara twilight had already fallen, and lights were beginning to glitter along Ankara's streets and avenues.

As she stood transfixed the last notes of a muezzin's chant reached her ears from below, sounding phantom in the high clear air, and Mrs. Pollifax thought, *I must remember this moment,* and then, *I shall have to come back and really see this country.* Yet she knew that if she did come back it would be entirely different. It was the unexpected that brought to these moments this tender, unnameable rush of understanding, this joy in being alive. It was safety following danger, it was food after hours of hunger, rest following exhaustion, it was the astonishing strangers who had become her friends. It was this and more, until the richness of living caught at her throat, and all the well-meant security with which people surrounded themselves was exposed for what it truly was: a wall to keep out life, a conceit, a mad delusion.

She was still standing there when Sandor walked up the steep path. It had become quite dark; she realized with a start that she had been standing there for a long time. "Is that you?" he said, peering at her. Little squares and stripes of light lay behind him on the path, formed by the shuttered and open windows of the surrounding houses.

"Yes," she said. "Where have you been?"

He said buoyantly, "I have biggest good luck! The twice-a-week bus for Yozgat leaves at dawn. It will be hot, cheap, very crowded. I went to Taksim Square to be sure—already the families sleep there waiting."

"Bus?" said Mrs. Pollifax wonderingly. "But won't the police be stopping the busses too?"

"When you see the busses you understand," he said cryptically. "Only Turks take them—tourists never!—and they buy tickets distantly ahead. But wotthehell, for big price I get four tickets to Yozgat."

He said modestly, "For a little extra I come too. You need me for the translations."

She turned and looked at him gratefully. "Oh yes, we do need you, Sandor, but I scarcely dared hope—Aren't you wanted by the police too, Sandor? Who are you really?"

"A scoundrel," he said with a grin. "Who are *you*, really?"

She laughed. "Obviously I ask too many questions."

"That you do, yes." He shrugged. "Be comfortable, don't itch. It is like a story of Nasr-ed-Din Hodja who went through the East many hundreds of years ago. His stories live everywhere. One of them is that Nasr-ed-Din was walking a road one dark night when he saw three men coming toward him. 'Oho,' he thinks, 'they may be robbers' so he jumps over a wall and hides behind a rock. The three men see this and are curious and they too jump over the rock and go to him. 'What is wrong?' they ask. 'What are you doing here?' And Nasr-ed-Din sees the truth of it—that they are not robbers— and he says, 'Oh gentlemen, I will tell you why we are all here. I am here because of *you*, and you are here because of *me*.' "

Mrs. Pollifax smiled. "A most philosophical parable. Are there more of them?"

"*Evet*. Another story is that Nasr-ed-Din said he could see in the dark. Someone said to him, 'That may be so, Nasr-ed-Din but if this is true why then do you always carry a candle at night?' Nasr-ed-Din said, 'Why, to prevent other people from bumping into me!' "

Mrs. Pollifax laughed delightedly.

Sandor took her arm. "More I tell you another time. Please, go inside now before we are heard speaking English. Tomorrow at dawn we go to Yozgat."

CHAPTER 11

HAVING BEEN OFFICIALLY HIRED AS THEIR GUIDE, Sandor took them over with stern authority. He allowed them to sleep until three o'clock in the morning and then he prodded them awake. "For you to be real peasants you get up now. You will do rest of the sleeping in Taksim Square, please. Like others."

The three of them arose stiffly from their floormats. They would have to wash on their way down the hill, at the public well, Sandor told them; Madrali was bringing them tea and fruit for their breakfast. They would also be carrying their lunch on the bus with them—it was already packed in a basket: two jugs of water and the remains of their evening meal. He produced a small cardboard suitcase that looked as if it had been possessed by a dozen other people first. Into this Mrs. Pollifax packed her suit for Magda to wear, and Colin added a number of spare reels of film. His cameras he insisted upon carrying in a string bag. Mrs. Pollifax again checked her pantaloons for the wads of money and Magda's passport, all secured with large safety pins. Her flowered hat was presented to Mr. Madrali with instructions to dispose of it, as well as her useless, emptied purse.

They started out in the pale light of dawn, and at the base of the hill wrung Mr. Madrali's hands, thanked him and were once again on their own, a little more secure in their new identities but a little less secure at being on the street.

"I think I could get to like these baggy pants," said Mrs.

89

Pollifax, lengthening her stride. "Is my headgear properly wrapped? Are you sure we're all right, with everything where it should be?"

"Good, very good," Sandor said gravely. "Except slower—please! You act like American. Dressed as you are dressed you come from a small village—do not walk so fast, so happy, and please—stay behind us men!" He shrugged apologetically. "Not for myself, you understand, who know precisely who you are but for the role, the act. Anatolian women, they work hard, say nothing. And to wear the shawl pulled so across the mouth you must be very shy, very small village. You understand?"

"All right."

Sandor added, "You do not look so Turkish as the other lady, you see."

"Oh—sorry," she said contritely, falling still another pace behind him and Colin.

"And stop talking English," contributed Colin, delivering the final snub.

Magda's eyes were gleaming over her veil with amusement. "It worked," she said.

"What did?"

"You look properly cowed and snubbed now. Your shoulders droop, you look shamed and subservient."

Mrs. Pollifax said in a peevish undertone—she really had been feeling expansive—"It's all very well for you—he said you look the part."

"Touché," said Magda with a throaty little laugh that reminded Mrs. Pollifax she would be delightful company under more relaxed circumstances. They turned down a broad, tree-rimmed boulevard lined with buildings so modern that Mrs. Pollifax might have forgotten she was in the Near East but for the sight of goats being herded down a side street, and a flock of turkeys being driven screeching, wings flapping, across an intersection.

When they reached the square they learned what Sandor had meant about bus transportation to Yozgat. A bulging and ancient wooden vehicle stood beside the curb—"It's early," explained Sandor—and around it squatted dozens of families who looked as if they had been waiting all night long. Sandor reminded them they must not speak to anyone, not even to one another, but smile and keep smiling agreeably. They silently sat beside the others. After about an hour the driver of the bus came whistling across the boulevard, unlocked the bus and began shouting orders to the passengers to bring their suitcases to him for storage on top of the bus. A policeman wandered over and watched, then alarmed Mrs. Pollifax by asking to see the cards of identity and the bus tickets of everyone waiting to leave.

"Do not panic," whispered Sandor. "Steady does it."

When the policeman reached Mrs. Pollifax she concentrated on looking as small and submissive as possible. "Yurgadil Aziz," he said musingly, as he examined her identity card. "Bilet?" he added, holding out his hand.

Sandor arose, spoke easily in Turkish and produced four bus tickets from his pocket. Mrs. Pollifax gathered that she had been asked for her ticket, and because the tickets had all been sold days earlier the possession of one precluded any of them being newly arrived Americans wanted by the police. The tickets were handed back, the policeman moved on, the bus driver shouted, passengers shouted, and like lemmings rushing to the sea they swarmed onto the bus. A child vomited. A pig squealed. Those without seats sat on the floor. Men and women laughed and congratulated themselves upon being there, and the trip to Yozgat was begun.

Seven hours and one hundred and thirty-eight miles later the bus jolted into Yozgat following innumerable stops to cool and refill an aging radiator, exercise children, revive fainting women and change a tire. After seven hours in such cramped quarters any disguises had become academic: everyone aboard knew that three of the passengers did not speak Turkish but no one appeared to even question the fact or to care. They were foreigners and therefore guests. Whether they were Yugoslavs or Rumanians or Bulgars—apparently no one even conceived of their being Americans—they were treated charmingly: smiled at, handed grapes, peaches and sweets and offered seats on the aisle several inches farther from the dust that billowed in through the open windows. Nevertheless the seven hours seemed endless and Mrs. Pollifax could feel only compassion for the majority of the passengers who were bound for Sivas. "When will they get there?" she asked Sandor.

He shrugged. "Six o'clock, eight o'clock, midnight, who knows? Only Allah. But do not worry, they are having the time of their lives."

"Magda isn't. She's looking horrible again."

"I will help her. Then I make discreet questions about the gypsies you seek," said Sandor. "There are always men in the square, and in a town like this everyone knows everybody else's business. I have thought further. In Yozgat there will not be many cars, and few gasolines. It will be less prominent to rent a horse and wagon. Wotthehell, okay?"

"What the hell okay," said Mrs. Pollifax with a smile, and as the bus halted in Yozgat square, honking its horn dramatically, she stood up and looked for Colin, who had become trapped in the aisle in back of her and could only wave and shrug.

Magda was helped from her seat by Sandor, and the three of them made their way to the front of the bus. Sandor jumped down first, followed by Magda, who almost fell into his arms, and Mrs. Pollifax stepped down behind them, lifted her head to look around her at Yozgat, and abruptly stiffened.

A man had separated himself from the cluster of people on the pavement, and had stepped forward to scrutinize each passenger as they dismounted. Now he was staring attentively into Mrs. Pollifax's half-concealed face; his glance moved to include Sandor and then fell upon Magda who swayed on Sandor's arm.

The man was easy to recognize because of his small pointed white goatee. She had in fact already exchanged glances with him once, across a crowded Istanbul living-room. It was Dr. Guillaume Belleaux.

Now he stepped forward and spoke to Mrs. Pollifax in Turkish, his eyes a little amused as they rested on the wisps of hair that escaped her shawl. Before she had even faced the problem of replying his hand moved and he whipped back her scarves to expose her face. "Mrs. Pollifax, is it not?" he said carefully. "Precisely the woman Mr. Carstairs asked me to take care of—which I plan to do at once!"

Mrs. Pollifax stepped back in dismay.

"And your two companions would be Madame Ferenci-Sabo and Mr. Colin Ramsey of Ramsey Enterprises." He lifted an arm and waved to someone across the street. "I am aware that you know karate," he continued smoothly. "One move toward me and the gun that I hold under this newspaper will kill you."

"Wotthehell," said Sandor, but whether he was shocked at being mistaken for Colin, or by news of the gun, it was impossible to guess.

Mrs. Pollifax sighed. To get safely away from the searching Ankara police they had endured those seven uncomfortable hours on a bus only to walk into Dr. Belleaux's waiting arms. It did seem unfair, and exactly the sort of thing to blunt initiative.

"The car is coming—patience, please," said Dr. Belleaux. "We have only a few streets to go, and I advise you to enter the car quietly." He turned and looked at Colin, who stood paralyzed on the bottom step of the bus, gaping at him. He said sharply, *"Hareket etmek—cabucak!"*

Colin closed his mouth—he had looked singularly stupid with it open—and to Mrs. Pollifax's astonishment he snarled, *"Evet, evet,"* in a low surly voice and walked stiffly and angrily away.

For a moment Mrs. Pollifax was incredulous and then it dawned upon her that Dr. Belleaux had not recognized Colin; he had looked for two women and a man and he had found them without realizing that four of them traveled together now, or that Colin was also a member of the party. Colin, bless him, had understood this perfectly, and at once.

She and Sandor exchanged a long glance, and then the car drew up behind the bus and Dr. Belleaux said sharply, "Get in, please!" He held the door open. "No, Mr. Ramsey, sit in front, please, where I can shoot you if you prove difficult."

To enlighten confused Sandor Mrs. Pollifax said coldly, "Allow me to introduce you. I believe this is Dr. Guillaume Belleaux—you are, aren't you?—the leader of the gang who tried to kill us on the road to Ankara." The impact of this on Sandor was appreciable: she saw his eyes blaze before they went studiously blank. "The gentleman beside you," she added tartly, "is Stefan, who works with Dr. Belleaux and abducts people and drugs them, too."

Ignoring her Dr. Belleaux leaned forward. "Leave now, Stefan, the bus will remain here for some time, I think. You know the way? That street over there, then left and a sharp right."

The car turned off the square, past a corner store whose signs read CIKOLATA—SIGARA—KOKA-KOLA (*I can read that*, thought Mrs. Pollifax numbly) and down a cobbled street that soon turned into a solidly packed dirt road of the most primitive type. "Where are we going?" inquired Mrs. Pollifax.

"Not far," confided Dr. Belleaux; his voice was friendly and gracious; he was obviously a born host. "It seemed wisest to rent one of Yozgat's abandoned houses, while we waited for you. We have expected you, of course, and I guessed you would have to arrive in some kind of disguise, or not at all, with the police looking for you so assiduously. But of course the police have never known that you were coming to Yozgat. It gave Stefan and myself *such* a pleasant advantage!" He leaned forward. "To the right now, Stefan. When you reach the house drive the car around to the rear. I don't wish it seen from the road." To Mrs. Pollifax he said in a kindly voice, "I have a gun, you know. Several, to be exact. It is best if you understand now that there is nothing for you to do but relax and tell me all I wish to know. Then we shall understand one another—once you understand your situation."

They had pulled up beside a low, dusty stone house with a shuttered and empty look. The nearest house stood a quarter of a mile away. Stefan backed, and then drove up a rutted track to the back yard and cut the engine.

Dr. Belleaux said, "Assim is inside—blow the horn once, lightly. We will tie their hands tightly for the walk into the house."

When the door shut behind them it closed out all sunshine. Not even the shutters betrayed lines or threads of light. They stood in darkness until Dr. Belleaux lighted a candle, and then a lantern. "In here," he said and they were pushed into one of the two back rooms.

This was a room like a shed; obviously animals had once shared it with humans during cold winter nights. The floor was of beaten earth; a pile of old hay still filled one corner and there was a strong smell of must and manure. Once there had been a rear door but it had been bricked in but not whitewashed. Three straight wooden chairs occupied the center of the room; one by one they were tied to them, first their hands behind their backs and then their ankles. When this had been accomplished by Assim, whose face was sullen and cruel, Dr. Belleaux beckoned his helpmeets into the other room and Mrs. Pollifax could hear them speaking together in Turkish in low voices. She said softly, "Magda—you are all right?"

Magda lifted her head and wanly smiled. "For the moment, yes. But to come finally to Yozgat, to be so close—" She stopped.

Sandor said in a voice choked with rage. "You understand even I have heard of this Dr. Belleaux. I am still shocked, still in a daze. There must be the way to get free. Must!"

Mrs. Pollifax sighed. "Such as what?"

"There's Colin."

Mrs. Pollifax said gently, "What can he do? He doesn't even know where we are."

"Surely something!"

"What?"

Sandor was silent and then he said angrily, "I don't know!"

"He doesn't know where we've been taken," repeated Mrs. Pollifax, "and if he did, what could be done? He is alone, completely inexperienced and unaccustomed to violence."

"Since meeting you he has seen a little," pointed out Sandor dryly, and as the voices broke off in the other room he said, "We cannot just die like trussed pigs, there has to come a moment, just one—" He was silent as Dr. Belleaux re-entered the room.

"Ah there you are!" said Dr. Belleaux, as if he had absentmindedly misplaced them. "We have just been consulting on the arrangements. I have an interest in a small archaeological dig not far from here—you will be buried there tonight." He chuckled. "In a few years you may be dug up and acclaimed a real archaeological find!"

"Very amusing," said Mrs. Pollifax tartly. "And Mr. Carstairs? What will you tell him?"

Dr. Belleaux smiled charmingly. "Why, that I searched everywhere but that you and your little party had vanished from the face of the earth!"

"He really cabled you about me?" Mrs. Pollifax asked curiously.

Dr. Belleaux leaned against the wall and looked down at her in a friendly fashion. "Oh indeed yes, just last evening, and giving a very full description of you—which of course proved at once how dangerous you are to me! He had cabled me earlier about Henry Miles, naturally, but failed to mention you. It was fairly simple to dispose of Miles as well as the first chap whom I believed Miles was replacing, but I really had no idea who you worked for. When you stole Ferenci-Sabo from under my very nose—in full view of my friends—I still had no idea you worked for Carstairs, can you imagine?"

"How stupid you must feel," she agreed pleasantly. "For how many years have you been a double agent?"

"It scarcely matters," he said modestly. "Actually I've been what is usually referred to as a 'sleeper.' That is, held in abeyance for something truly worthwhile. Although I won't say I've not taken advantage of my privileged situation to cast a few stones," he confided charmingly. "An innuendo here, a lifted eyebrow there—" He obligingly lifted an eyebrow. "But Ferenci-Sabo's defection was big enough to bring orders for me to capture her at any cost, including my usefulness as a friend of the Americans and the Turks." He smiled. "However—happily for me—the cost looks very small indeed. By tomorrow I can look forward to resuming my *very* pleasant life in Istanbul again. For now, however," he concluded, his voice changing, "I must get to work."

"Hain," growled Sandor.

"What does that mean?" asked Mrs. Pollifax.

"It means traitor," said Dr. Belleaux indifferently. He walked over to Magda and stared down at her. "Now what I should like to learn first," he said firmly, as if he were interviewing her for a job, "is just why the Americans have been brought into this, and how they were contacted. I find that—shall I say very suspicious?" He continued looking at Magda. "Lift your head!" he demanded sharply.

Slowly Magda lifted her head. "I want you to talk," he said in a suddenly cold and chilling voice. "You will tell me why and how you contacted Mr. Carstairs. You will tell me where are the papers you brought with you, and why you insisted on coming to Yozgat."

"No," said Magda.

Dr. Belleaux began to hit Magda across the cheekbones, methodically and viciously, and Mrs. Pollifax closed her eyes so that no one would see the tears she wept for Magda. Back and forth went the hand—one, two, one, two—but in his savagery Dr. Belleaux had miscalculated Magda's stamina. Her head suddenly went limp—she had mercifully fainted.

"Bastard," shouted Sandor.

Dr. Belleaux turned toward Mrs. Pollifax, and as she realized that her turn was next she closed her eyes again. A sudden picture of her sunny apartment in New Brunswick, New Jersey, flashed across her mind and she thought, *Is anything worth all this?* and then she opened her eyes and met Dr. Belleaux's gaze steadily. He stood over her, eyes narrowed, fist lifted, and she prayed for courage.

CHAPTER 12

STEPPING DOWN FROM THE BUS COLIN WAS APpalled at the sight of Dr. Belleaux in conversation with Mrs. Pollifax. It jarred all his senses; he had not glimpsed Dr. Belleaux at his house in Istanbul but he recognized him from newspaper pictures, and it was a shock to see him in the flesh, and here of all places. His second reaction was one of wild relief: everything had to be all right after all, Mrs. Pollifax had been wrong about Dr. Belleaux, and Dr. Belleaux had come to tell her so; and then he realized that this couldn't be so, the man had no business meeting them here in Yozgat, and as his eyes dropped to the newspaper that Dr. Belleaux held in such a peculiar position he instinctively realized there was a gun hidden there. It was all very disappointing and unnerving, and for a moment he thought he was going to be ill. He stood frozen to the bottom step of the bus while behind him voices rose in protest at his blocking the exit.

The protests inevitably drew Dr. Belleaux's attention; he turned, saw Colin staring and spoke sharply to him in Turkish, telling him to get moving, to go away. Colin was astonished to remember that he was in disguise, and was even more astonished to realize that he had not been recognized. He stammered, *"Evet—evet,"* and walked away from the bus and then across the street.

There he stopped, suddenly aware that he had nowhere to go. He realized that Mrs. Pollifax and Magda and Sandor

98

had just been captured, and he felt an acute sense of loss. It seemed incredibly unjust after all they'd gone through. He thought dimly of shouting for the police and then he remembered that in joining Mrs. Pollifax he had placed himself beyond such conventional avenues of complaint. This was a chilling thought. There was no one at all to help—no one except himself, of course, and there was nothing he could do. Nothing at all. He saw Dr. Belleaux lift his arm and wave to a man seated in a parked car, saw the driver nod, turn the car and drive up behind the bus. Over the top of the car he saw the heads of his three friends as they climbed inside, and he heard the doors slam. Then the car pulled out and turned down the street next him. It passed quite near but the shades had been drawn in the rear and he saw only the driver. It was Stefan.

At that moment Colin understood that he was about to see his three friends vanish from sight—he would never know where they went, or see them again. He suddenly found this even less tolerable than his panic.

Furiously he glared at the people around him: wraith-like, ancient men slumped half-drowsing on benches in the shade; a woman dispiritedly sweeping with a twig broom; a boy pulling a loaded donkey across the road, the bus driver loading the bus with what looked like a sack of mail. At the corner he saw a narrow, fly-specked cafe open to the square—one sign said CIKOLATA—SIGARA; another advertised KOKA-KOLA. His glance fell to three old and dusty bicycles leaning against the wall, their owners apparently inside the shop. The car had just turned into the street beside that shop; a cloud of dust rose as it vanished.

Without thinking, and purely from instinct, Colin ran across the street, snatched up one of the fallen bicycles, mounted it and peddled madly down the street into which the black car had turned. There were shouts behind him but he ignored them and peddled faster. He couldn't see the car but he knew it was there because its dust filled his nostrils and choked his throat. He had no idea where he was going, or even why, he knew only that he musn't be separated from the group in the car.

He became increasingly aware that he was being pursued, and the shouts following him annoyed him. He peddled past low rock walls, a dusty vineyard, little houses with peeling stucco until the cobbles came to an end and he faced two unpaved roads. As he hesitated his most immediate pursuer peddled up beside him: it was, of all things, a girl, who proceeded to upbraid him in a flurry of noisy Turkish.

Despairingly, in English, he cried, "I can't understand you, I don't understand a word!"

The torrent went on and then suddenly, her lips open, the girl stopped in mid-sentence, her eyes enormous. "But you speak English! You're not Turkish!"

"Yes, I'm English, and I've lost my friends, they're in that black car that drove down this street, and I'm terribly sorry to have—" He too stopped in mid-sentence. "But I say—you speak English too!"

She said impatiently, "I go to college in Istanbul. But what are you doing in such clothes? Are you a sociologist studying our customs? You are dressed like a peasant!"

"I must find that car!" he said urgently.

"The car went to the left, do you not see the dust?" she said calmly.

He peddled a few feet and turned. "Look, I'll return your bicycle, I promise you. Or come along if you doubt me, but I have to follow that car!"

"I will go with you," she said firmly.

They peddled together up the road to the left. Houses were set close together in a long row like small boxes; a rivulet of dirty water ran down one side of the road in a hollowed-out trough. The street turned at an angle, displaying another length of soiled houses and dirt road and Colin had to swerve to avoid a goat. A donkey brayed from under a dusty tree. Here and there sat worn men; there were no women to be seen. The houses thinned, and he saw no car but at the last house on the road—isolated and at some distance away—there still lingered a faint cloud of dust.

"They are in that last house," the girl said. "Why are they staying there? It has been unoccupied for years. Are you sure they're in there? I will wait while you go to the door."

Colin climbed down from his bike. "It's not that simple," he said, turning to look at her and discovered that it was a mistake to look at her a second time. His first impression had been of a slightly plump and rounded young woman with a bland and candy-box sort of prettiness. Between first and second glance all clichés had vanished: she was exquisitely lovely. Her face *did* belong on a candy box: one of those fragile old Victorian boxes that dripped paper lace. Her skin was flawless, her lips full, sensual and pink, her eyes huge, round, heavily lashed and a curious shade of vivid blue that by contrast brought to life the very ordinary shade of brown hair. He frankly stared. "What's your name?" he asked.

"Sabahat Pasha. What is yours?"

"Nazim Aziz," he said absently.

She laughed. "What? But you are not Turkish!"

He flushed. "Actually it's Colin Ramsey but— oh hang it all, do go now," he said, parking his bicycle against a crumbling wall. "I'm going to walk the rest of the way."

"Go?" she said, and laughed. "How can I ride two bicycles back to town? And why do you not ride up to the door and make sure your friends are there?"

"Damn," he said, and looked at her helplessly, at her wide naïve eyes, and warm sympathetic mouth. How could he possibly explain the situation to her? It was impossible.

"Something is wrong," she said, watching him. "You are in some kind of trouble." The laughter had gone from her eyes, leaving them grave.

"Yes," he admitted. "But it's not a police matter," he added hastily. "They're all Americans, and calling the police would—well, prove very embarrassing."

"Americans!" she exclaimed. "Americans here in Yozgat? Oh but I would love to meet them! What brought them here to Yozgat? Are they also studying the customs?"

"We came to—" He stopped. With extraordinary clarity he suddenly remembered why they had come to Yozgat, and it occurred to him that help might be available after all. He said excitedly, "Sabahat, tell me. Are there gypsies camping in or near Yozgat?"

She looked startled and then thoughtful. "There were a number of them camped just outside of town for a few days. I know because they read the palms of many of my friends. But I hear they left yesterday, going south, and now there is only the man with the dancing bear."

"And is he a gypsy too?"

The girl laughed. "But of course—only the gypsies have dancing bears!" She looked at him, puzzled. "But he is very dirty, very soiled," she pointed out.

"Do you know where he stays?"

She nodded. "Beyond the mosque, on the road leaving town. I have seen his wagon. Also his dog." She shivered distastefully.

He said recklessly, "Please—if I ride the bicycle back to town with you, could you direct me to the road leading to the gypsy with the dancing bear?"

"You wish to *see* him?" she said in astonishment.

"I must."

She recoiled, obviously disturbed, and then she looked into his face and suddenly laughed. "Your moustache has slipped! It is crooked!"

He grinned. "I'm not surprised, the blasted thing itches, too." He felt for it with two fingers and began to peel it off, the girl watching gravely, as if the most important thing in the world at the moment was to learn how moustaches were removed.

But he had underestimated her intelligence, which had continued to assess and appraise him as they talked. She nodded suddenly, as if she had made up her mind. "Come— I will take you myself to the gypsy," she said. "You would not be able to speak to him if you found him, would you? I'm sure my friend won't mind if I borrow the bicycle a little while longer."

"I say—that's awfully kind of you," he said gratefully, and then he heard himself ask, "Your friend—is it a girl or a boy?"

She glanced over her shoulder at him with amusement. "It is my girlfriend."

Colin turned his bike around and followed her back down the road into town. When they reached the square the bus had finally departed and in its place stood a small dingy cardboard suitcase and a string bag. "Good grief—my cameras! And Magda's suitcase!" he gasped. He had forgotten all about them. He stowed them away on the back of the bicycle, and with Sabahat in the lead they set out to look for the gypsy.

*   *   *

The gypsy's cart stood at some distance from the road, half-hidden within a grove of scrub and stunted trees. His campfire burned in a circle of stones, guarded by an ugly, ferocious-looking dog. "He must be at home because the bear is tied up to the wagon," Sabahat said, and added nervously, "But the dog is not tied."

"I'll go first," Colin told her. "Stay well behind, until I can get him to tie the dog. If he's there."

They didn't need to shout; they had no sooner left the road than the dog sprang up, growling, snarling, barking, baring his teeth in a terrifying manner, and when this did not send Colin into retreat the dog flew toward him as if to devour him. Colin stood still, his heart hammering. The gypsy appeared suddenly from the woods and stood watching, saying nothing, his gaze hostile, arms folded.

"I must talk to you," Colin shouted. "Call off your dog, will you?"

Behind him Sabahat bravely translated, her voice quivering only a little.

The gypsy spoke to the dog and the dog slunk away, head down, eyes still on Colin. Colin and Sabahat wheeled their bicycles nearer.

"Be careful," Sabahat said in a low voice, "I am sure he would like to steal the bicycles—see how he looks at them! Gypsies will steal anything."

"You'll translate?"

She nodded, eyes huge.

"Tell him I come to Yozgat to find the gypsies who were here yesterday. Ask if he knows them."

Sabahat translated and the man shrugged and replied. "He says if you give him money he will tell you anything you wish to hear."

Colin said sharply, "I don't want him to tell me anything I wish to hear, I want the truth. I'm looking for a family of gypsies who were supposed to be here in Yozgat."

Sabahat and the gypsy exchanged words. "He says he wonders what you want of a gypsy family."

"I have a message from a friend of theirs."

"A friend of the *gypsies*?" faltered Sabahat.

"Yes. Tell him I come to Yozgat with that friend; she

crossed the border into Turkey with them. Now she's in trouble and needs help."

The man's glance was sharp and inscrutable but when he had listened to Sabahat his face grew less closed. With much casualness he asked what the name of that lady might be who was a *gorgio* yet a friend of the Rom.

"Magda," said Colin, not daring to speak her well-publicized last name.

The man shrugged. He said he knew of no such person, nor anything of the gypsies who had been in this place.

"What you say is true?" whispered Sabahat.

Colin nodded. What could he produce to prove that he was speaking of Ferenci-Sabo, or had really known her? He suddenly remembered the passport photographs he had taken of Magda, and kneeling down beside the suitcase he burrowed through it. "Ah," he said triumphantly as he found two discarded pictures of Magda, and he carried one of them to the gypsy. "Magda," he said.

A flash of recognition lighted the man's eyes but as quickly as it arrived it was replaced by suspicion. Colin groaned. "Blast it, now he thinks I'm the police no doubt. Sabahat, I want you to tell him something very carefully, translating it for him sentence by sentence."

She nodded.

"Tell him Magda is in Yozgat. Tell him Magda was captured an hour ago. Abducted. Kidnapped."

Sabahat looked at him in astonishment. "Abducted?" she gasped.

"Please—tell him," Colin begged. "Tell him if he does not believe me then he can go and see for himself. You know the name of the street?" he asked Sabahat. "Tell him that, too. Tell him she is in an abandoned house, two men took her there."

The man's eyes had narrowed, and he looked at Colin so quickly that Colin wondered if the man did not know a little English after all. The man began to speak.

Sabahat said breathlessly, "He says the gypsies you look for left here late yesterday and began moving south on the road to Kayseri. And—" She gasped. "And he says he would like to see the house in Yozgat of which you speak."

Colin drew a sigh of relief. "Thank God—then he does know what I'm talking about!"

The gypsy began speaking again. "He asks you," said Sabahat, "to sit down with him on the steps of his caravan and tell him more clearly what has happened. He also wishes me to tell you that unfortunately he has no guns."

Colin said gravely, "Tell him I am a believer in nonviolence, anyway."

"Are you really?" cried Sabahat breathlessly. "Oh but so am I! So are all my friends here and at college," she said with shining eyes. "Tell me, have you experienced any—what are they called—love-ins?"

Colin shook his head regretfully. "I'm sorry, no."

"You have spoken of such violent things—abductions, kidnappings—it is very difficult to imagine this. Who could do such a thing? Is it one of my own people who has done this to your friend?"

"Actually a Frenchman, I think," Colin said.

"So *many* foreigners in Yozgat?" she exclaimed. "Oh how my friends would love to know of this, you cannot imagine our hunger to speak to people from other lands. The summers in Yozgat are so very long, so very hot and tedious."

Colin abruptly halted on his way to the caravan. "How many friends have you in Yozgat?" he asked thoughtfully.

"Why, there are about twelve of us home from college." Her eyes suddenly slanted mischievously. "You are thinking of the same thing? You must be! I know you are!"

Colin looked at her and she looked at him, communication leaping between them. He thought he had never met anyone so perceptive unless it was his sister Mia.

The gypsy grunted—he had been waiting patiently for them. He spoke in a rush of Turkish to Sabahat, who leaned forward courteously to listen. When he had finished she nodded and smiled at Colin. "It's all right—he says he will trust you. He says he remained here, behind the others, to wait for the woman Magda and to guide her to the other gypsies. He says if you are the police then he will kill you with his knife. Otherwise he will help us."

"Us?" Colin said in surprise.

She smiled at him gravely. "If I abandon you now, how shall I ever learn if you succeed?"

Colin grinned. "Somewhere I've heard that before," he said dryly. "All right, let's make plans. This won't be easy but tell him I'm awfully glad to have him on my side."

"Me, too?" she asked boldly, her cheeks turning pink.

"You too," he said, smiling.

From where Colin and the gypsy crouched, the town seemed far away. They had crossed fields and then empty land to reach the shed behind the house in which Magda, Mrs. Pollifax and Sandor had been hidden. They had been taken here at twenty past one o'clock; it was now half-past three in the afternoon. Ahead of them nothing stirred, and they slipped around to the front of the shed and inside. The darkness of its interior was welcome. They had come to reconnoiter, to make certain that the three were still in the house.

The gypsy pointed to the car and Colin nodded. They crept from the shed across the barren yard to its shadows, where the gypsy unsheathed his long knife and slashed each tire. When he sheathed his knife again they moved to the wall of the house and sat down under one of the two shuttered windows, pressing their ears against the wall.

A moment later Colin was hearing Sandor's voice repeat over and over, *"Ikiyuzlu . . . Ikiyuzlu . . ."* It was a word Colin had heard his uncle use several times and so he was familiar with its meaning, which was hypocrite, or more literally, his uncle had explained, someone who wore two faces. Then Sandor abruptly said, *"Canavar . . ."* and was silent. He at least was still alive.

The gypsy had begun sitting back on his heels to stare at the wall above their heads, studying it fixedly with half-closed eyes, and now he astonished Colin by running his hands lightly over the surface. Colin saw that a seam ran up and then down the wall in the shape of a doorway that had some time ago been bricked-over, but clumsily. The gypsy's fingertips came together at one particular brick, he braced himself, leaned a little, and lifted the brick out with his hands. Just as quickly he put it back and turned to smile at Colin. It was a smile of infinite triumph and satisfaction. At once they both began to check the surface for other loosely mortared bricks, and together found a dozen, all in the area that had once been a door. Like all the houses in Anatolia, this one had been built as a child would build a house of blocks: by simply placing one row of sun-baked adobe bricks on top of the other without resorting to beams or joists, and then at a later date a thin veneer of cement or stucco had been added. The veneer had peeled away from most of this abandoned house, exposing the crumbling mortar; sun and wind had done the rest.

Having discovered the dozen bricks that were loose, the gypsy brought out a knife for each of them and without a word spoken they began to gently pry loose the mortar surrounding the other bricks. They worked for half an hour and then Colin glanced at his watch, touched the gypsy's arm and whispered, "Sabahat."

The man nodded, signaled that he would remain, and Colin crept away to hurry back into town and meet Sabahat.

After waiting fifteen minutes for Sabahat, Colin grew restless. She had instructed him to wait in the cafe, where he would be less vulnerable to curious passersby; on the other hand she had also pointed out that women never entered cafes in Anatolia, and so he must watch the window—grimy and fly-specked—for her face and her signal. He was reduced to sitting on a bench near the door and nervously fingering the identity card in his pocket and then his reapplied moustache.

The men seated around him in the cafe looked as if they had been turned into stone fifty years ago—he swore none of them had moved since he entered except the two men playing chess in the corner; twice they had reached forward to move a chesspiece. The others remained oblivious: unblinking, lips closed around hubble-bubble pipes, eyes blank. Colin felt he might have stumbled blindly into an opium den.

Two more men entered the cafe, followed by a third, and in fascination Colin watched to see how they would distribute themselves. The first to enter neither nodded nor spoke but moved to a corner and joined the silent ones. The second sat down and spread out a newspaper. The third said in a clear voice, "Raki," and turned to survey the room.

Colin gasped. The man who had just violated the silence

was his uncle Hu. There he stood in his usual faded blue
work shirt and khaki shorts, looking around him for a face
that interested him, his streaked hair and moustache bleached
a shade closer to white after a week in the sun. Colin's first
instinct was to dive under a table and hide, and then he remembered that he was in disguise. He met his uncle's gaze
without flinching.

But this time he should have hidden. His uncle's trained
photographer's eye slid over him, looked away and then
slid back. A moment later, glass of raki in hand, Uncle Hu
strolled over and sat down at the table nearest Colin.

From the corner of his mouth, very pleasantly, he said,
"Do you mind telling me what the devil you're doing here in
Yozgat in that absurd moustache?"

Colin froze. He wished desperately he knew Turkish well
enough so that he could get up, mutter something appropriate to an Anatolian peasant, and stalk away insulted.

"Of course I don't mean to trespass," his uncle continued
in a mild voice, "but I have just spent one of the most horrible nights of my life in the local jail here. It seems that
anyone driving a Ramsey Enterprises vehicle is being
stopped by the police, searched and detained while the Istanbul police are consulted. I have been released—at last—
because I don't answer to the description of the young
sandy-haired chap they're looking for, who is traveling in
the company of a woman wanted for questioning in some
fiendish murder in Istanbul."

Colin said desparingly, "Let's go outside."

"Delighted," said his uncle. "I wondered at the time
why I chose such a gloomy place to celebrate the end of
my incarceration."

The sunlight was almost blinding. "How did you recognize me?" asked Colin miserably.

His uncle said witheringly, "My dear chap, you're my
nephew. Oh, don't look so worried, I can't imagine anyone
else recognizing you. I have a remarkable memory for faces,
you know. When I saw you I thought, 'Those are Colin's
cheekbones and eyes, in fact that looks precisely like Colin
in peasant clothes and moustache.' And then—considering
the circumstances, which have been somewhat jarring—I
thought, 'Why *not* Colin in peasant clothes and moustache?'

Now for heaven's sake tell me what the hell you've been up to while I've been in Erzurum. I don't mean to mix my metaphors—"

That was his uncle, thought Colin, concerned over metaphors in the midst of a trying situation. "Yes, sir," he said as they sat down on the bench outside the cafe. "Well, you see it's this way, sir—and I'll have to talk quickly— three friends of mine have been kidnapped here in Yozgat and are in a house about a mile away."

"I see," said his uncle. "Well, of course then you've got to get them out," he said without so much as a blink of the eye.

"Yes, sir," Colin agreed with a faint smile.

"One of these—er, friends—is the alleged murderess the police are looking for?" he inquired.

"Yes, sir—but she didn't murder anyone, Uncle Hu. I was with her when Henry's body was left in the studio—your studio—" He stopped. He could not think of any possible way to explain the events of the past two days to his uncle. "It's all quite complicated," he added weakly. "Can't you just pretend you didn't see me and go on to Istanbul?"

His uncle considered this. "I could," he said reflectively, "but not without hearing your plans first. You have made plans, haven't you?" he said sharply.

"Yes, sir."

"Stop sir-ing me, I'm not your father." He frowned. "The thing is, I won't have you going to jail—horrid places, Turkish jails. I could volunteer. I'm not without experience in this kind of rescue operation—I was in the war, you know, and God knows these jails are to be avoided, your mother would never forgive me if—"

At that moment Sabahat hurried around the corner, gave a cry of relief at seeing him, and cried breathlessly, "We're ready—it's all settled! Yozgat's leading poet is going to read a poem of welcome—the same one he made up for the Premier's visit two years ago!—and the Greek Orthodox priest is going to say a prayer!"

"Poets? Priests?" said Uncle Hu with interest. He looked appreciatively at Sabahat and then at Colin. "I say—you do seem to be managing something rather well, do you mind terribly if I come along, too?"

CHAPTER 13

MRS. POLLIFAX SIGHED AND OPENED HER EYES. She had fallen or been pushed to the floor, still tied to the chair, so that her cheek rested on the hard earthern floor and any spontaneous movement was impossible. She heard Sandor say in a loud voice, *"Canavar ..."* and she knew that something had happened to awaken her but she did not know what. From the other room—the door was open—she heard Dr. Belleaux say in a low voice, "Bring the serum out anyway. We'll have to risk its killing her, there's no other way ..."

"Magda," said Mrs. Pollifax in what she believed to be a loud clear voice, but realized a second later was only a whisper. She could not see Magda from where she lay—it must be Magda they had taken into the other room. She could see Sandor's feet not far away, the toes springing from his torn sneakers, but she could not see any more of him without lifting her head, and her head was on fire with a ribbon of pain that moved from cheekbone to brain. Concussion, she thought drowsily; could cheekbones have concussion? and then she drifted off again into unconsciousness.

When she next opened her eyes it was with the impression that she was in danger of being attacked by rats. She realized that she had been dreaming of rats gnawing their way through the wall, and for a moment, awakening, she thought she might still be within her nightmare because she distinctly heard rustling noises in the wall. *But that is definitely*

110

a rat in the wall, she thought, listening. *I'm not losing my mind after all. I've regained consciousness!* There was not a great deal of reassurance in this thought because her circumstances had not changed. She remained huddled on the floor in the semi-darkness, her cheek pressed to the earth, the murmur of voices ebbing and rising from the other room. But she discovered that she was feeling better: still stiff and bruised but no longer aflame. She knew that it was blood she could taste when she licked her lips, and her nose ached, but it no longer throbbed, and the ribbon of pain had vanished. She dared to hope that no bones had been broken.

The voices from the other room were audible and she tried to make sense of them but she was still too blurred. She heard ". . . having gone to Bulgaria to help with security arrangements for the Festival of Youth. . . ." and then, "You had intended from the first to go to the British Consulate in Istanbul?"

"Not alone, no . . ." That was Magda's voice, oddly toneless. "But I had not expected to be looked for so quick or so—so accurately. I could not make trouble for my gypsy friends."

Gypsies, thought Mrs. Pollifax, frowning. Surely Magda ought not to be speaking about gypsies to Dr. Belleaux? She wondered what time it was, and as she licked her dry lips she wondered if she might call out for water. She felt very tired and dull. She tried to focus her eyes on Sandor's disreputable sneakers and then she tried to practice thinking very carefully. She supposed it was Thursday—no, no, it must still be Wednesday, late afternoon or early evening of their arrival day in Yozgat, and Dr. Belleaux had promised that presently they would be shot and carried off in the black car to an archaeological dig. That was not a very pleasant thought. She wondered if her body would ever be found and identified. Perhaps it was better if it wasn't, she reflected, since it would only prove extremely embarrassing to Mr. Carstairs and then of course there were her children. They were very nice children, Roger and Jane, but they would simply not understand how their mother came to be murdered in Turkey disguised as a native peasant woman. Nor would she be there to soften the explanation that between

Garden Club meetings and her hospital work she had acquired this interesting little sideline as a CIA courier. It was not the sort of thing one could explain, certainly not to Jane at least.

But as her sluggishness diminished Mrs. Pollifax remembered that there was even more to be concerned about: there was Dr. Belleaux. The thought of Carstairs continuing to trust the man so appalled her that it jerked her to full consciousness at last, and in time to hear Dr. Belleaux say quite clearly, "You have been described as a defecting Communist agent, Madame Ferenci-Sabo. You are known to the Russians in this manner, too. But actually you have worked for the Americans all these years, is this not true?"

Mrs. Pollifax gasped, terrifyingly alert at last. It must have been drugs they had administered to Magda to force her to speak. Words overheard earlier came back to her . . . *we'll have to risk its killing her, there's no other way* . . . Not an ordinary drug then, but one of the truth serums.

No no no, she screamed, but no sound came from her throat and it was part of this nightmare that she could move her lips and her tongue yet make no sound. She began to struggle against the ropes that held her bound, frustrated by her helplessness to halt or delay Magda's confession to being a double agent.

"Yes, that is true," Magda said in reply, still in that cold, toneless voice. "I have been—am—a counteragent."

As Mrs. Pollifax sagged defeatedly she caught a glimpse of Sandor now, his head turned to listen. She noted the welt across his cheekbone and the gag stuffed into his mouth—he must have gone on shouting—and she thought, *Now he knows what Magda is, too.*

"I see," Dr. Belleaux said, and his voice shook a little, betraying his excitement at discovering that his wild suspicion was a literal fact. He drew a sharp breath and when he spoke again there was barely suppressed triumph in his voice, as if he knew he stumbled upon a masquerade so outrageous and so sinister that its ramifications would be felt everywhere—and especially on his own career, thought Mrs. Pollifax bitterly.

"Please tell me next how you notified the Americans after your extraordinary escape from my two men."

"I took money. Stefan had left some on the table, Turkish

lira, and I took it. One of the gypsies in Istanbul sent a cable for me."

"And the address to which you sent it?"

Magda recited a cover address in Baltimore.

"Thank you!" said Dr. Belleaux cheerfully. "Thank you very much. Now I would like to discuss with you where you have hidden the missing document, the top secret paper you brought out of Russia with—"

He stopped abruptly. Mrs. Pollifax had heard it, too, an indefinable sound of movement outside, of something brushing the front door. Now she realized it had been a knock; it was repeated.

"What the devil!" exclaimed Dr. Belleaux. "Stefan!"

"*Evet,*" said Stefan calmly. "It is only a young girl, I saw her come. She has a notebook and pencil."

"She will have heard voices. Answer and get rid of her. Assim, hide the hypodermic. Cover the woman so she looks ill."

Mrs. Pollifax had been holding her breath. Now she expelled it and cleared her throat, testing it to see if her voice worked yet. If she could only scream—Practicing, she said in a small, hoarse voice, "Someone—is—at—the—door."

She at least captured Sandor's attention; he made a frustrated rumbling noise in his throat and she saw him strain at his ropes. Stefan was unbolting and opening the front door. Mrs. Pollifax heard a clear young voice speak with a rush of enthusiasm and charm. But the words were Turkish—she had forgotten they would be. Mrs. Pollifax formed a scream in her throat. "Help!" she called out raspily. "Help! Help!"

Dr. Belleaux murmured something in Turkish in an amused voice, gave a little laugh and crossed the floor to close the door between the two rooms. With this act he blotted them out with finality.

Tears came to Mrs. Pollifax's eyes. "I'm sorry, Sandor," she said. "I would have liked to really scream but it's my voice. I can't."

Sandor rumbled again in reply. "I'm sorry you've been hurt and tied up and gagged," she told him, because it was important to practice speaking in case a second opportunity arose. "I'm sure you must be extremely sorry you ever joined us, but you must have overheard enough to realize this is something more important than any of us individually. It's the only attitude I can suggest," she added primly. The tears had run down her face to mingle with the dried blood on her cheeks. "I can only tell you—oh that rat in the wall is annoying," she cried furiously. "It's not enough that we're surrounded by human rats, there has to be—" She turned her head toward the outside wall.

Her gasp was almost as audible as her attempt to scream, for the wall was literally disappearing before her eyes. Sunshine was entering the dark room, inch by inch, as brick after brick was tidily, efficiently and very hastily removed by a pair of large brown human hands. Mrs. Pollifax could not believe it: either her vision or her mind had been seriously affected and she was hallucinating. Within seconds a space appeared large enough for a pair of shoulders, and at once a pair of shoulders blocked off the light that had bruised and stabbed her swollen eyes. The words that slipped from Mrs. Pollifax's lips were entirely unpremeditated; she said incredulously, "Wotthehell!"

It had the effect of turning Sandor's head immediately, and as he saw the light, the opening, and the man's head his eyes widened in shock. Clearly he saw it too, and she was not hallucinating at all. The man's shoulders cleared the opening and he lifted his head. Mrs. Pollifax had never seen him before; his face was dark, tough, crafty. He lifted a finger to his lips, and after pulling his legs through the hole he tiptoed across the room. He was followed by a second man, and he too was a stranger to Mrs. Pollifax, so that she became certain that she must have lost consciousness again and was dreaming some happy, wishful fantasy of rescue.

The second man was tall, lanky and dusty. As if by prearrangement he went to Sandor. Neither man expected them to be capable of walking. Ropes were quickly slashed. Smoothly Mrs. Pollifax was picked up, carried to the opening in the wall and tilted forward on her knees. Hands reached in from outside and gently grasped Mrs. Pollifax's bleeding fingers. She was half-pushed and half-pulled through the aperture into the blinding brilliant sun of a late afternoon that contained—of all things—a smiling Colin Ramsey.

"Colin!" she gasped.

"Yes," he said, grinning. "Isn't it wonderful?" As Sandor was pushed out into the sunshine Colin raised both arms and waved at someone she could not see. The tall, sandy-haired man followed Sandor out of the hole and the dark, fierce-looking one began swiftly replacing the bricks.

"You'll have to walk several yards before you can rest," Colin said firmly. "We have to get you to the front corner of the house, and we have only three minutes to do it."

She understood nothing of this except that it was obviously not a dream, and that it was being managed with infinite precision so that she need to do nothing at all. Nothing except walk, which was nearly impossible, but if Colin said it had to be done she would do it. Her feet felt like stumps, bloodless and lifeless, and her knees kept betraying her. Colin supported her, and the sandy-haired man supported Sandor, and slowly they reached the cover of a bedraggled grape vine at the corner of the house. Here the third man caught up with them and crouched down behind them as they waited.

A van drove slowly up the empty street. *Colin's van?* thought Mrs. Pollifax, bewildered, but that had been abandoned in Ankara. The van pulled up in front of the house. Half a dozen young people in western clothes leaped down from the rear and began unloading—it couldn't be possible—trays of fruit and food, jugs of water and huge armfuls of bright flowers. A man in the robes of a priest climbed down from the driver's seat and joined them; Mrs. Pollifax saw that they were going to walk up to the house in which she had been captive.

"Oh, stop them!" she whispered, and then, "Magda's in there!"

"We know that," Colin said calmly. "Sabahat knocked at the door a few minutes ago saying she was taking a census. She reported three men and an invalid woman in the front room."

"Sabahat? Census?" repeated Mrs. Pollifax dazedly.

"Now," Colin said to the sandy-haired man. The stranger nodded and walked down to the empty van and backed it up the cart track to Mrs. Pollifax and Sandor. "Get in quickly," Colin told her.

They fell clumsily into the rear, and then the van backed

down into the street, this time pointing toward town, the motor kept running by the tall stranger. Colin and the dark gypsy-looking man moved toward the house, and incredulously Mrs. Pollifax leaned out to watch. The young people and the priest had absolutely vanished—into the house, realized Mrs. Pollifax disbelievingly—leaving the door wide open. Inside, it looked as if a party was in full bloom—and into this melee walked Colin and the gypsy.

A moment later they backed out carrying an unconscious Magda between them. A girl joined them, laughing and calling over her shoulder to the young people behind her. For one incredible moment Mrs. Pollifax saw Dr. Belleaux swim to the door like a salmon fighting his way upstream. A crowd of laughing youngsters accosted him and pulled him back. Furious, he stretched out his two hands toward Magda, face livid, and then someone placed a plate of grapes in those outstretched hands, a garland of flowers was lowered over his head and slowly he was sucked back into the living-room, overwhelmed by currents too strong for him.

"What on earth—!" cried Mrs. Pollifax to Colin as the two men placed Magda in the rear of the van.

Colin grinned. "It's a love-in. Dr. Belleaux is being smothered with non-violence." He turned and grinned at the girl. "This is Sabahat, whose idea it was—Sabahat Pasha. Sabahat, ask Sebastien to sit up front and take us to the gypsies now, will you?"

"How do you do," Sabahat said, smiling at Mrs. Pollifax. "I'm so glad you are safe." She spoke to the gypsy in Turkish and then extended her hand to Colin. "I will make certain the three men do not get away for as long as is possible. I cannot promise much but it may help you a little," she told him gravely. "*Allaha ismarladik,* Colin Ramsey."

He shook his head. "Not for long, Sabahat," he said, firmly holding on to her hand, "You know I'll be back. In the meantime how can I thank you?"

She dimpled charmingly. "But my friends have always wished to meet such a scholar as Dr. Belleaux—there is no need to explain the situation to them. You are giving them a big day, and it is I who should thank you!"

He grinned. "Fair exchange then." He released her hand and shouted, "Okay, Uncle Hu, let's go!"

As the van roared into life and raced down the street Mrs. Pollifax exclaimed, "Did you call that man *Uncle Hu*?"

"Quite a lot has happened," Colin said modestly. "Yes, that's Uncle Hu. Letting him help seemed the least I could do, he's already spent one night in jail because of us, which places him beyond the pale. This is the van he drives—he was on his way back from Erzurum. The chap with him is a gypsy named Sebastien. I picked him up before I ran into Uncle Hu, he has a dancing bear and he stayed behind the other gypsies to wait for Magda."

Mrs. Pollifax looked at him in amazement. "Colin," she said, "you're an extraordinary young man."

He returned her glance, looked startled, and then a slow smile spread across his face. "Yes," he said with an air of discovery. "I believe I am."

CHAPTER 14

THEIR PRECIPITOUS FLIGHT FROM YOZGAT WAS IN-
terrupted by Sebastien, who somewhat desperately
reminded them that he had a horse, a dog, a wagon
and a dancing bear to be retrieved. Colin crawled up front to
the window and held a three-way conversation, the translations supplied by his uncle, but he crawled back to report that
Sebastien was adamant: he could not go any further without
his menage. They stopped briefly beside the road at the place
where the gypsy had made camp; Sebastien looked for several moments at Uncle Hu's map, then marked a cross on the
road, halfway between Yozgat and Kayseri.

Uncle Hu said, "He tells me the gypsies will be somewhere near the cross he's marked, and camping within sight
of the road because they expect him to follow."

"And will he follow?"

"He'll hope to catch up with us by dawn."

They thanked Sebastien profusely for his help, Mrs. Pollifax gave him money from the wad pinned inside her baggy
pants, and they resumed their breakneck trip south. Watching Mrs. Pollifax return the bills to their hiding place Sandor
said with a weak grin, "The Bank of Pollifax, eh?"

"Hold still," Colin told him sharply, trying to wrap gauze
around Sandor's bleeding wrists. "Uncle Hu always drives
like this," he explained resignedly, "although I rather imagine he's trying to cover as much ground as possible before

dark. You've no idea how black it gets out here on the plateau."

"No street lights," said Mrs. Pollifax brightly. "What time is it now?"

"Nearly eight. One hour until dark. There," he said, tying the last knot on Sandor's bandage and turning to Mrs. Pollifax. "Hold out your wrists. I do hope you've had tetanus shots recently, they're a pulpy mess."

"Shouldn't you do Magda's first?"

He laughed shortly. "Why? She has an advantage over you, she's unconscious. But her wrists aren't in such bad shape, they must have been untied when they drugged her." He looked soberly at Mrs. Pollifax and said, "By the way, I think it's time I ask how much Dr. Belleaux found out while he held you three captive."

Mrs. Pollifax sighed. "Nearly everything."

"Good God!"

She nodded. "This time they gave Magda a different sort of drug. They tried first to make her talk without it, but she wouldn't." To Sandor she said frankly, "You know who she is now, too."

He dropped his eyes. *"Evet."*

"But does Dr. Belleaux know about the *gypsies*?" Colin asked. When Mrs. Pollifax nodded he shook his head. "What a foul piece of luck! That means he knows precisely where we're heading, or soon will. Everyone in Yozgat can tell him the gypsies have gone south."

Mrs. Pollifax felt it unnecessary to reply. The fresh air that had revived her was beginning to stupefy her now, and the wonder of being rescued was being replaced by fresh worries. She felt very weak, and a little nauseous—a reasonable reaction to what she had gone through but still inconvenient. If choice were given her she would without hesitation choose a hospital—even a nursing home would do, she thought wistfully—where she could bleed quietly between clean sheets, rouse only to sip nourishing liquids and to observe new ice packs being placed on bruises and swellings before drifting off into an exhausted sleep. Instead she was rocketing off across the bumpy Anatolian plain again, in a rather dirty van, while she sat on an extremely dirty floor holding on for dear life and adjusting to the realization that they were still in danger, and probably greater danger now because Dr. Belleaux knew everything about them.

Aloud she said, "Dr. Belleaux is going to be feeling very nasty, I think—he's just lost that elegant Istanbul life of his that he planned to get back to tomorrow, after burying us in some ruins."

"He almost did bury us," growled Sandor.

Mrs. Pollifax considered this and nodded. Yes, there was a great deal to be said for such an attitude: without Colin they would be dead now, in which case there would be no choice left them at all. *I'll feel sorry for myself later,* decided Mrs. Pollifax, and firmly put aside thoughts of rest to take charge again. "What weapons do we have, Colin?"

He looked amused. "You've gone professional again— I'm relieved. I still have Stefan's pistol, with three shots fired."

"They did not search me," Sandor said, bringing out the gun he had periodically waved at them. "But wotthehell, it's empty," he added sadly.

"Uncle Hu may have something," Colin said. "Of course he may no longer carry a gun because he's never been attacked on these trips by anything more than a goat. If he ever slows down I'll ask him."

But his uncle Hu gave no sign of slowing down, in fact as the road grew more atrocious his speed seemed to increase, as if he regarded the stones and gullies and potholes as an affront to an unblemished record. Magda had been rolled into a rug and braced against one wall; she was almost to be envied. If this was Wednesday, thought Mrs. Pollifax nostalgically— and she thought it was—she would be wheeling the hospital's bookcart at home, and tomorrow she would normally be having her karate lessons with Lorvale.

Except what was normalcy, she wondered; in Mr. Carstairs' world she was not even overdue yet, and certainly he had no idea that in cabling Dr. Belleaux her identity and description he had signed her death warrant for so long as she was in this country and at the mercy of Dr. Belleaux's considerable resources. She was neatly trapped indeed. Each new detail that Dr. Belleaux learned only inflamed his desperation as well as his ambitions: *he must* find them. They could escape him for the moment by going to the Turkish police and appealing for help, but this would at once cancel all hope of Magda fleeing the country; she would again become public property to be schemed over, fought over, questioned, requestioned and exploited. But even worse. Mrs. Pollifax suspected that by surrendering to the police they would become sitting targets for Dr. Belleaux instead of moving ones. It would take time and patience for their shocking charges against Dr. Belleaux to be investigated and proven, and while facts were checked they would be confined to some small area accessible only to the police, many of whom had already been charmed by that genius of criminology Dr. Belleaux. What would the headlines be then, she wondered: Mysterious Explosion Wipes Out Political Prisoners? or Fire Sweeps Wing of Prison, Five Dead? It was too risky to contemplate.

In any case, without passport and wanted for Henry's murder, Mrs. Pollifax could certainly not leave the country herself now. Her hopes had to be concentrated exclusively on Magda. If Magda could somehow be spirited beyond the border then she at least would be free—and she could communicate with Carstairs. . . .

She said, "How far are we from the nearest border, Colin?"

"Which one?"

"Any—except Russian," she amended.

Sandor answered. "From Greece about two hundred and fifty kilometers. From Syria maybe three hundred."

Mrs. Pollifax shook her head. "Too far. Where is the nearest airport then?"

Colin looked at her in dismay. "I believe there's one at Kayseri, about fifty miles south of us. But surely—"

"Do you think they'd dream of our risking an airport?"

Colin said, "No. Yes. Oh I don't know!"

She pointed out gently, "Every day that goes by will give Dr. Belleaux a better chance to find us. It's Time that's our worst enemy, but if we move boldly—"

Sandor turned and looked at her with interest.

"But that's such a reckless *gamble*," protested Colin. "What if it shouldn't work?"

Sandor grinned. "She's okay—she's got the crazy spirit. Except wotthehell I never expect it from such a person." He looked at Mrs. Pollifax appreciatively and his grin deepened.

Abruptly the van began a wild braking, jumped and came to a grinding halt. Uncle Hu slid open the window that in this van separated the cab from the rear. "Radiator," he said, gesturing ahead.

Thick clouds of vapor curled up from the hood of the van, obscuring the road. "She's boiled dry," he added unnecessarily.

"Oh dear," said Mrs. Pollifax, and she too crawled to the door of the van to follow Colin and Sandor outside.

"It will take time, maybe half an hour," Ramsey said, meeting them there. "Can't put cold water into a hot radiator or she'll crack, you know." He disappeared into the van and handed out sterno, pans and water jug. "Set it up, Colin," he said. Nodding pleasantly at Mrs. Pollifax he held out his hand. "How do you do. Hugh Ramsey's the name."

"Emily Pollifax," she said briskly, shaking his hand.

"That woman in there who was drugged—she hurt, too?"

"Bruised mainly. Still unconscious."

"Might as well leave her inside then. Turkish?"

"Uh—" Mrs. Pollifax opened her mouth and then closed it. "European," she said weakly.

Ramsey nodded and began pouring water carefully into two pans. "Damn nuisance, this," he said in his mild voice.

Colin drew out his gun. "I'll take a look at the road behind us," he said, and moved off toward a cluster of rocks and disappeared, soon to appear on top of the largest one. "No one on the road for miles," he called. "Where are we, Uncle Hu?"

His uncle shouted back, "We passed through Osmanpasa and crossed Kizil Irmak. Must be about forty miles out of Yozgat, sixty from Kayseri."

Mrs. Pollifax was looking at the sun that hung suspended over the range in the south, possibly the same mountain range she had seen from Ankara the evening before. A curious lavender and gold light bathed the wild land around them, the beginnings of a dusk that would suddenly terminate in darkness. They could ill afford this stop, she thought, and hoped the gypsies were not far ahead. "Do you see any signs of a gypsy camp?" she called to Colin.

He turned and looked in the other direction. "No."

The first two pans of water were boiling. Ramsey and

Sandor carried them carefully to the front of the van, opened the hood and the radiator, and poured the hot water inside. Ramsey put his ear to the radiator. "So far so good," he said, returning to pour more water. "Drink some while we have it," he told Mrs. Pollifax, handing her a cup.

"Do *you* know about an airport at Kayseri?" she asked him hopefully.

"Oh yes, there's an aerodrome there. They've limited service, but in summer there are several flights a week to Ankara and Istanbul."

Colin had climbed down for a drink of water and he joined them now, explaining, "Mrs. Pollifax is determined to get our passenger"—he jerked his head toward the van,—"moving toward England."

"Yes," said Mrs. Pollifax firmly, and asked, "Is it true—absolutely true—that if we succeeded in getting her to Kayseri she would show her passport there, but *only* there, no matter how many changes she made en route out of the country?"

Both Colin and his uncle nodded. "Quite right," Ramsey said. "She'd go through Passport Control and Customs at Kayseri, but at Istanbul she'd be considered *In Transit* and would be issued an In Transit card during her wait in the air terminal. This she'd give up as she boarded her plane for London or Paris or whatever."

Mrs. Pollifax's interest increased. This was it, of course—if it could be done. If they could get Magda to Kayseri. If she could walk through Customs without being challenged and stopped. There would be that one terrifying moment of inspection, but if she passed . . .

Watching her Colin said indignantly, "Mrs. Pollifax, you don't even know the plane schedules!"

His uncle Hu startled them both by saying, "I've got one in the van. I try to keep very up-to-date on plane, train and boat schedules, especially in summer when everything opens up in this part of the country. The water's hot—pour it in, will you? I'll go and look."

A fresh batch of water was on the fire when he returned carrying a shoebox stuffed with folders. "I've got it," he said, waving one. "It's the Van-Istanbul flight, Turkish airlines. Three days a week, Mondays, Wednesdays and Fridays departing Kayseri eight o'clock in the morning and arriving in Istanbul at eleven, with an asterisk denoting that this plane makes connections with the noon flights to Paris and London."

"Well!" said Mrs. Pollifax, delighted. "I believe I'll go inside and see if Magda's stirring yet."

"Take her some water," Colin suggested.

"You'll need a flashlight inside," contributed Ramsey, and crawled in ahead of her. Colin and Sandor followed and they all surrounded Magda, who remained inert.

Mrs. Pollifax felt her pulse. "She seems all right," she said doubtfully. "She just doesn't wake up."

Colin said peevishly, "How you can even think of her taking a *plane* in a day or two!"

Uncle Hu said firmly, "If she can swallow water we must give her some before she becomes dehydrated. I'll hold her up. Give me the cup of water, and Colin shine the flashlight on her face."

Magda was lifted, still encased in her rug and still inert. The flashlight was turned on and Uncle Hu leaned over Magda with the cup.

The cup suddenly slipped from his fingers to the floor.

"What is it?" gasped Mrs. Pollifax, who could see Ramsey's face. "Colin, he's ill—do something!"

Uncle Hu shook his head; his face was white. *"Who is this woman?"* he demanded in a shaken voice.

"It's Magda," said Mrs. Pollifax, regarding him with astonishment. "We're taking her to the gypsies."

He shook his head violently. "Where did you find her? Where does she come from?"

They stared at him stupidly.

His voice rose. "Don't you understand I know this woman? She was supposed to have died in Buchenwald twenty-six years ago!"

Mrs. Pollifax said blankly, "Magda?"

"Not Magda!" He leaned forward and peered into the flashlit face. "I tell you she's Alice. Alice Blanche."

Something stirred in Mrs. Pollifax's jaded mind; a face, a recognition, a memory. Alice Blanche . . . but Blanche meant white in French, didn't it? Alice White—Alice Dexter White. . . . "You know her?" she faltered.

He nodded. "During World War Two, when I escaped from prison camp. She hid me for three months in Paris—occupied Paris. She—I—" He hesitated and then said simply, "She was very beautiful and very brave. Reckless, really. I thought she was captured and imprisoned. Charles said so. The Hawk said so. Red Queen said so. You must think I'm talking absolute gibberish," he said, looking up at Mrs. Pollifax. "She was an agent, you see."

Mrs. Pollifax nodded. She said quietly, "She still is. That's why you never found her."

He said in an appalled voice, "You can't be serious."

"I'm very serious. Surely you're aware that you've just helped rescue some rather controversial people from a house in Yozgat, and that we may be pursued even now?"

"Yes, but it's you, isn't it? Surely it's you who—"

Mrs. Pollifax said briskly, "Only superficially. It's this woman they're really after, and it's this woman we must get to Kayseri for a plane out of this country. If you've had time for newspapers on your trip you may have read about a certain Magda Ferenci-Sabo."

He nodded. "Yes, that defecting Communist agent."

Mrs. Pollifax glanced down at the still-unconscious Magda and said with a sigh, "Meet your defecting Communist, Mr. Ramsey. Now we really must leave before it grows any darker or we'll never find the gypsies. Is there enough water in the radiator now, Mr. Ramsey?"

"Yes," said Ramsey, still staring at Magda. "Good God!" he exclaimed again, incredulously, but he turned off the flashlight and followed them out without delay. They poured the last of the boiling water into the radiator. The sun had set with finality while they were inside the van, and twilight was rapidly replacing the long shadows. It would be dark in a matter of minutes.

Darkness came, and nothing existed for them except the twin beams of the van's headlights on the stony road ahead. Yet lacking darkness Mrs. Pollifax realized they would never have seen the gypsy camp, for it was the light of the campfire that drew their eyes: like an earthbound star it shone at some distance off the main road, made luminous by the opaque blackness surrounding it. Seeing it, Colin's uncle turned off the road and they bumped and jolted over a cart track of eroded earth and scrub.

"More dogs," groaned Colin as there mingled with the roar of the van the sound of howling cur dogs.

"Never mind, these are Magda's gypsies," Mrs. Pollifax told him warmly. "We've found them." Peering out she saw that there were two fires, one at either end of a camp laid out in a rectangle among rocks and a few stunted trees. Six or eight wagons had been drawn up to this rectangle, and Colin's uncle drove neatly into the middle before he brought the van to a halt.

"We're here," he shouted over his shoulder.

"Yes," said Mrs. Pollifax gratefully, and opened the rear door and stepped down.

Gypsies had appeared like shadows and formed a ring around the van. "Good evening," said Mrs. Pollifax eagerly. "We've brought you Magda, we're looking for—"

She stopped uncertainly. She realized that the gypsies formed a solid circle around her of folded arms, grim eyes and hostile faces. Not one of them moved but their eyes almost physically forced her to step back in retreat. For one nightmare moment Mrs. Pollifax wondered if they were going to stone her to death. She had never met with such an impenetrable wall of hatred. Something was terribly wrong.

Then from the shadows a voice said, "Good evening, Mrs. Pollifax!"

Dr. Belleaux strolled smiling into the circle of light followed by Stefan and Assim. "You mustn't expect a welcome here, Mrs. Pollifax. I arrived twenty minutes ago by helicopter and warned these people about you." He said softly, with a helpless shrug, "They already know that you've hidden Magda in the van, and that you've beaten and drugged her. I've told them they mustn't kill you but they are so very aroused, what is one to do?"

CHAPTER 15

FOR A MOMENT MRS. POLLIFAX THOUGHT SHE WAS going to faint but that would have been too merciful; she did not faint. He had said what, *helicopter*? It smacked more of black magic against this wild, primitive backdrop of sky and stars and earth lighted by campfires. "It's not true!" she flung at the gypsies and looked into their high-cheekboned, mahogany faces but her glance met no response. The frozen mute hostility did not waver; she felt whipped and shriveled by their bitter and accusing eyes.

"He lies!" she protested. "You musn't believe him! We're Magda's friends!"

Behind her Colin said in a shaken voice, "I don't think they speak any English, Mrs. Pollifax."

"Not at all?" she cried passionately. She swung around. "They must know Turkish then! Sandor—Mr. Ramsey—translate, tell them quickly!"

"Good God, yes," murmured Uncle Hu, and stepped forward. He began to speak Turkish, and had produced several sentences when Stefan calmly walked up to him and hit him with his fist, sending him unconscious to the ground. At the same moment Mrs. Pollifax heard a startled grunt from Sandor on her right—he ducked his head and ran.

The wall of gypsies shattered. With shouts the men took off after Sandor into the darkness while the women tightened the circle around Mrs. Pollifax, presumably to prevent her bolting too. "No no no!" cried Mrs. Pollifax, impatiently stamping her foot. "Do understand! Magda is our friend, that man lies!"

One of the women spat contemptuously.

"Inglis," said Mrs. Pollifax in case her baggy pants and shawls confused them. "You must listen to me! We're all in danger from that man!"

Half a dozen women climbed into the rear of the van. There were murmurs and gasps at the sight of Magda, and then little crooning sounds as she was lifted and brought out. Gently they carried her toward the more distant camp-fire, with Dr. Belleaux following and speaking to them, obviously pointing out each bruise and cut to them in an effort to whip them into a new fury of hatred.

Mrs. Pollifax looked at Stefan, who looked at her mockingly. She turned and looked at Colin, who was leaning over his uncle. She wondered if Sandor had been caught yet. She wondered how she could possibly make the gypsies understand that if they didn't act quickly they would all be killed, and their beloved Magda too. She wondered how long it would be before Magda regained consciousness. That was something only Dr. Belleaux knew, and he seemed very confident that Magda's ability to speak was not an imminent threat.

He was shouting to Stefan now, and to complete the irony he was shouting in English. "Tie them up," he called. "We can use the helicopter radio to contact the police. They can be here by dawn."

Police—dawn; what was he planning, she wondered as Stefan pushed them forward. Could Dr. Belleaux really afford to call in the police, or didn't he plan to be here when they came, or would they all be dead when the police arrived? Certainly by dawn he must expect to retrieve whatever document Magda had stolen from the Communists; if he already had this he would not be here. Now that he had established himself to the gypsies as Magda's protector was he counting on this to provide him with the gypsies' confidence? She was growing too tired to think.

Stefan led them past the second campfire where Magda had been placed between blankets. A dark, tousle-headed boy of nine or ten sat cross-legged beside Magda, watching a woman apply ointment to Magda's face wounds. The woman looked up at Mrs. Pollifax as she passed and hissed, *"Baulo-moosh!"* Clearly it was an epithet of the worst kind.

At some distance from the fires their bandaged hands were tied behind them again, and then to the trunk of a stunted, low-flying tree that looked curiously Japanese in its distortion. From here they could no longer see the van or Uncle Hu lying in the dust beside it. They could see one gypsy wagon and the silhouette of a horse grazing behind it in the shadows. They could see the fire and Magda's blanket-shrouded body, the woman and the boy. Beyond this circle of light the far-away cliffs were etched sharply against the deep blue night sky. The silence of the plain was almost complete except for the sound of the wind and an occasional muffled shout from the men who searched for Sandor.

"Well," said Mrs. Pollifax dispiritedly.

"Well," said Colin.

Stefan had disappeared. The boy who had been sitting beside Magda at the campfire arose and walked across the open space toward Mrs. Pollifax and Colin. He chose a position a few yards from them and sat down, cross-legged, to watch them now. He watched without expression, his face impassive. Two young men suddenly appeared and began to search Mrs. Pollifax and Colin. Their faces were dark, swarthy and leanly handsome, their hands expertly light. When they came upon Mrs. Pollifax's wad of money and unpinned it they shouted and held it high to show the boy, who laughed delightedly. The two young men added Colin's watch and pen to their treasure and happily walked away.

"A pretty kettle of fish," said Colin savagely.

Mrs. Pollifax said wearily, "I don't know how to make them understand. Surely someone here must have heard English spoken once or twice?"

Colin said doggedly, "They undoubtedly speak Bulgarian— no mean accomplishment—since they came from across the border. Of course they speak Romany, and probably some Hungarian as well, and a little Turkish. But even if they understood some English our dear old friend Dr. Belleaux got here first."

"But why would we come here to the gypsies at all—with Magda—if we'd beaten and drugged her?"

"For the same reason Dr. Belleaux came here: to get from the gypsies what Magda left here with them. In his case before she wakes up and calls him a bloody liar."

"If only she would—right now!" said Mrs. Pollifax with feeling. "She'd give one long loud scream at sight of him, and tell these people who he is in their own language, and—but will Dr. Belleaux *allow* her to wake up?"

"No, but he can't very well kill her in plain sight of her friends." He added wryly, "At the moment I'm more worried about us. Nobody here would mind seeing *us* killed, and we haven't one single state secret up our sleeves to prolong our living. He can keep Magda drugged while he goes to work on the gypsies but we're only nuisances. I keep remembering Sebastien. He was going to hitch up his wagon, feed his dancing bear and follow us, remember?"

Mrs. Pollifax said gloomily, "But he didn't expect to find us before dawn, and it can't be midnight yet, can it? And it's more likely he fed his bear and then decided to curl up and sleep for a while. I'd rather put my money on Sandor, who at least—"

She stopped. The gypsies were bringing Sandor back into camp. One large and muscular gypsy carried him slung across his back like a slab of venison. In a long procession the men crossed their line of vision, passed the campfire and disappeared. "Unconscious," she said despairingly. "Not even capable of explaining in Turkish to the gypsies who we are!"

Colin said soberly, "What do you think Dr. Belleaux has in mind—that is, if you can enter that mind of his at all?"

Mrs. Pollifax considered. "I can at least guess. With Magda he has two possibilities: either he will fly her off to Russia with whatever papers he mentioned, or he will kill her and fly off to Russia himself with the mysterious papers. He has that helicopter. I daresay it's provided him by the Russians, and he need only radio ahead and cross the border at some prearranged spot with very little risk of being shot down."

"Either possibility disposes of his pleasant life in Istanbul at least!"

Mrs. Pollifax laughed. "Don't be naïve, my dear Colin.

He can easily salvage his pleasant Istanbul life by saying that I murdered Magda."

"And risk a trial?" asked Colin. "Or am I being naïve again?"

"Yes, you are, really," Mrs. Pollifax told him. "Because by that time he will have seen to it that the gypsies kill *me*. Stone me to death, no doubt," she said tartly.

Stefan and Assim reappeared suddenly, carrying a trussed-up but still breathing Sandor. They knotted him to the tree as well—it was becoming heavily populated. Stefan said with a grin, "The gypsies hunt well for us, eh? We'll even let them kill you soon."

"Bring that other man here, too," said Dr. Belleaux, strolling in from the shadows. "The tall thin one. What is his name?" he asked Mrs. Pollifax.

"I don't think I'll tell you," she said coldly.

He shrugged. "It scarcely matters in any case." He regarded the tree with interest. "Perhaps this tree is the best solution of all for your demise, certainly less tedious than simulating knife murders for you all by the gypsies. A little kerosene sprinkled at the base of the tree, a match, a flaming tree and there would be no embarrassing traces left at all. The Turkish police," he added, "will be here by dawn. It is so very difficult to puzzle out how to dispose of so many of you."

Mrs. Pollifax said coldly, "You're very disappointing, Dr. Belleaux, you appear to have the mentality of a Neanderthal man—except I rather imagine I'm insulting the defenseless Neanderthal. I had expected something a little more imaginative, discriminating and subtle from a man of your obvious taste and background. You must be growing quite desperate."

Dr. Belleaux nodded. "It is a matter to which I must still give careful attention, Mrs. Pollifax," he admitted. "To me also it feels unpleasantly primitive. I naturally prefer the gypsies to kill you, as I think they will. But you have to be dealt with by dawn, which accelerates the pace. In any case you may rest assured that I will evolve a way of disposing of you all that will suit my own welfare—not yours," he added with a charming, if pointed smile. "Ah, you have the fourth one, Stefan—good! He is beginning to stir, and he speaks

Turkish, so gag him as well, please. Check all the knots, Assim, and then back to the helicopter."

Mrs. Pollifax said indignantly, "You must realize that Magda will never give you what you want."

Dr. Belleaux smiled. "Of course not, but the gypsies will. They believe what I tell them."

"I find it rather depressing to have been right about that," Mrs. Pollifax said to Colin.

Dr. Belleaux glanced at his watch. "I advise you to say your prayers," he concluded. "I shall be speaking again now by radio to the police in Istanbul, and by dawn the police should be rendezvousing here from all points of Anatolia."

"And you?" asked Mrs. Pollifax.

"I will be—elsewhere."

The three of them walked off into the darkness and vanished. The boy guarding them also got up suddenly and ran off into the shadows, leaving them alone.

"I'm terribly sorry, Colin," Mrs. Pollifax said with a sigh.

"If you're going to say what I think—don't," he told her coldly. "I was never—at any point—your responsibility, and you know that. I chose to come along, and I simply won't have you going all bleary and sentimental about me now."

She said gently, "And if I do, dear Colin, precisely what can you do about it?"

He said stiffly, "Well, I shall certainly think the less of you. I've no complaints—it's been a bit of a romp, you know."

She turned her head and looked at him. "I trust that you have the intelligence to realize that you're *not* a coward, and never have been!"

He grinned. "That's rather choice, isn't it? And how else would I have found out?"

The boy was returning. Again he came across the turf but this time he walked up to Mrs. Pollifax and looked into her face searchingly, and then from his pocket he drew out a small knife, leaned over her and cut the ropes at her ankles and wrists.

Colin said in astonishment, "I say—am I imagining things, or did he just—"

The boy fiercely shook his head, pressing one finger to his

lips. As Mrs. Pollifax stared at him blankly he beckoned her to follow him.

"But the others!" protested Mrs. Pollifax, pointing to Colin and Sandor and Mr. Ramsey.

The boy shook his head. His gestures grew more frantic.

"Go with him for heaven's sake," Colin said in a low voice. "You're not going to look a gift horse in the mouth, are you? If you make a scene he'll tie you up again!"

Torn between loyalty and curiosity Mrs. Pollifax followed him. Once she looked back, and at sight of her friends tied helplessly to the tree she would have gone back to them if the child had not tugged furiously at her baggy pants. What did he want, wondered Mrs. Pollifax and why was he doing this? She limped with him past the horses, around rocks and wagons—he was obviously hiding her from the other gypsies, and her curiosity had become almost intolerable when ahead of her she saw a tent pitched between two boulders. It was the only tent that she had seen in the camp. A light inside faintly illuminated its ragged edges and spilled out from its base. The boy pulled aside a curtain and gestured to Mrs. Pollifax to enter.

Mrs. Pollifax walked in. A lantern hung suspended from a tent pole, and seated cross-legged on a pillow beneath it was a square-shouldered gypsy woman. Hair threaded with silver hung to her shoulders, framing a square, high-cheekboned dark face. The eyes in the lantern light smoldered under heavy lids, and now they pierced Mrs. Pollifax like a laser beam.

The boy spoke rapidly to the woman, and she nodded. He beckoned Mrs. Pollifax to sit down in front of the gypsy, and Mrs. Pollifax stiffly lowered herself to the hard earth.

"Give me your hands," the woman said abruptly.

Mrs. Pollifax gasped. "You speak English!"

"Yes. The boy understands some but cannot speak it well."

Mrs. Pollifax's relief was infinite. "Thank heaven!" she cried. "I have tried—"

The woman shook her head. "Just give me your hands, please. Everything you wish to say is written in them, without lies or concealment."

"Without—" Mrs. Pollifax stretched out her hands, suppressing a desire to laugh hysterically. "If you insist," she said. "But there is so little time—"

"The boy tells me he has listened to you speak, and that my people have been lied to." She was gently examining the palms of the hands. "Your wrists are bandaged?"

"Yes. Like Magda's. The man in the white goatee did this."

"Hush." The woman closed her eyes, holding Mrs. Pollifax's hands in silence, as if they spoke a message to her. "You speak truth," she said abruptly, and opened her eyes. To the boy she said. "Bring Goru here at once—quickly! This woman does not lie, she lives under *koosti cherino*, the good stars." As the boy ran out she smiled at Mrs. Pollifax. "You are skeptical, I see."

"You can see this in a hand?"

"But of course—lips may lie but the lines in a hand never do, and I have the gift of *dukkeripen*. You are a widow, are you not? Your hand tells me also that you have begun a second life—a second fate line has begun to parallel the first one."

"All widows begin second lives," pointed out Mrs. Pollifax gently.

The woman smiled into her eyes. "With so many marks of preservation on that second line, showing escape from dangers? And a cross on the mount of Saturn, foretelling the possibility of violent death at some future date?" She allowed Mrs. Pollifax to withdraw her hand. "But I am clairvoyant as well," she went on. "When I hold a hand I get pictures, as well as vibrations of good or evil. I feel that you have come to this country only days ago—by plane, I believe—and I get a very strong picture of you tied to a chair—this is very recent, is it not?—in a room where there is straw in one corner, and a door that has been bricked-over."

"How very astonishing!" said Mrs. Pollifax.

The woman's smile deepened. "You see the waste of words, then. But here is Goru."

Goru was enormous—it was he who had carried Sandor back to camp slung over his shoulder—and he was made even larger by the bulky sheepskin jacket he wore. As the woman talked to him he looked at Mrs. Pollifax with growing surprise, and then with humor. He made a magnificent shrug, snapped his fingers and grinned. With a bow to Mrs. Pollifax he hurried out.

The woman nodded. "We shall have some sport with that *gorgio*," she said in contempt. "The man descended on us like a bird in his machine, and spoke knowingly and urgently about Magda. He knew everything! How is that?"

"He drugged her earlier tonight, with the kind of drug that produces confession," explained Mrs. Pollifax. "You will help us now?"

The woman's lip curled. "Wars. Assassinations. Drugs that make even a Magda speak—" She shook her head. "I do not understand this civilization of yours. Do not look so anxious for your friends, my dear—trust Goru. You came to this country to help Magda?"

Mrs. Pollifax nodded. "But I can tell you nothing that Dr. Belleaux has not already said—except," she added with dignity, "that Magda was not drugged when she spoke to me of going to Yozgat to find the Inglescus."

The woman smiled. "I am Anyeta Inglescu."

"Are you?" Mrs. Pollifax was pleased, and put out her hand. "I'm Emily Pollifax."

"The name of Inglescu was not mentioned by the man with the goatee," the gypsy added. "But I do not understand why he goes to such trouble to speak lies, to try and fool us."

Mrs. Pollifax said bluntly, "He wants the document Magda escaped with."

"Document?" said the woman curiously.

Mrs. Pollifax nodded. "Whatever it is that Magda brought with her out of Bulgaria and entrusted to you." She gestured helplessly. "Microfilm. Microdots. Code. She has told me nothing except that she preferred risking death to abandoning it."

Anyeta Inglescu laughed. "I see." Lifting her voice she called out, and the boy who had brought Mrs. Pollifax to the tent came inside. "Come here," she told him gently, and taking his hand said to Mrs. Pollifax, "This is what Magda brought out of Bulgaria and left with us."

"I beg your pardon?" said Mrs. Pollifax blankly.

"You did not know that Magda has a grandchild? This is Dmitri Gurdjieff. She smuggled him out of Bulgaria, and entrusted him to us when she went to Istanbul to get help."

"Grandchild?" faltered Mrs. Pollifax. "Dmitri?" She stared incredulously at the boy and then she began to smile and the smile spread through her like warm wine until it merged in a laugh of purest delight. She understood perfectly: she was a grandmother herself. But what exquisite irony for Dr. Belleaux, she thought, that the treasure Magda had smuggled out from the iron curtain was her grandson! "But this is marvelous!" she cried. Gesturing toward the darkness beyond the tent she explained, "Out there secret agents are fighting, bribing, even killing in their greed to learn what Magda brought out with her—and it's a small boy! Nine or ten?" she asked.

"Actually he is eleven," Anyeta said.

Mrs. Pollifax nodded. "I have three grandchildren myself, and you?"

Anyeta laughed. "A dozen at least." They both regarded the boy tenderly, and he smiled at them. "His father is a high Communist official, very busy, scarcely known to the boy, and now he has remarried. Perhaps you did not know that Magda had a daughter born of her first marriage. The daughter died last year. Magda could not leave without the child."

The boy suddenly spoke. "Is not all so."

"What is not all so?" asked the gypsy.

"There is more." He had grown quite pale. Reaching inside his ragged shirt he said, "Is time maybe to speak, Anyeta. There is more."

He pulled out a blue stone tied to a coarse string around his neck. "This."

Anyeta smiled and shook her head. "That is your Evil Eye, Dmitri. It's only part of your disguise. Turkish children wear them to ward off evil."

The boy stubbornly shook his head. "It's more, Anyeta. Grandma gave it me in Sofia."

Anyeta's eyes narrowed. "In *Sofia*?" she said in a surprised voice.

"Da. Is hollow inside—for secrets."

Anyeta drew in her breath sharply. "Allah protect us!" she said in amazement. "I see, I begin to understand . . . but what can it be?"

Mrs. Pollifax smiled. "Her social security, I think," she said, and the last piece of the puzzle fell into place.

CHAPTER 16

SUDDENLY GORU WAS BACK IN THE TENT, SPEAKING rapidly to Anyeta in an excited breathless voice. Anyeta's eyes narrowed, she nodded and turned to Mrs. Pollifax. "The man with the goatee has finished his work with the radio in the plane and is starting back to the camp. Goru asks you to return quickly to your friends and be tied up again."

In spite of Mrs. Pollifax's horror of being tied again she responded to the firmness and the urgency in the woman's voice. At the door of the tent she turned; Anyeta Inglescu had not stirred from her position. "You're not coming?" she asked.

The gypsy woman smiled. "I cannot walk," she said with a shrug of regret. "I have not walked in fifteen years."

"I'm sorry," said Mrs. Pollifax, surprised.

Goru had vanished; the boy Dmitri tugged at her arm nervously, and he guided her through the rocks back to the tree.

"What the devil!" cried Colin, seeing her. "Didn't you make a dash for it? Mrs. Pollifax, why the hell didn't you try to escape?"

She shook her head. "It's all right, Colin—really."

"All right? He's tying you up again!"

"Yes, I know." She turned and said carefully. "Listen but don't say anything, Colin, there isn't time. This boy understands English."

"*He* does?"

"Ssh," said Mrs. Pollifax as Dr. Belleaux came striding back.

He went first to the campfire and looked down at Magda, then he leaned over, felt her pulse, nodded and straightened. Seeing the gypsies emerge silently from their wagons he gestured them closer and began speaking to them. Eloquently he spread his arms, smiled, frowned, pointed to Magda, then to Mrs. Pollifax and Colin, his voice becoming increasingly edged with contempt and indignation. It was surprising, thought Mrs. Pollifax, how much could be communicated without a single word being understood.

"Born orator," growled Colin. "Real Hyde Park material."

"Can you catch any of it at all?"

"Just the word kill, which occurs with monotonous frequency," said Colin dryly.

Beckoning his audience closer Dr. Belleaux drew them away from the campfire toward the small group at the tree. Within minutes Mrs. Pollifax was surrounded closely and in danger of developing claustrophobia. At this point Dr. Belleaux suddenly drew out a knife; he seemed to be challenging one of the gypsies to use it, and to Mrs. Pollifax's surprise Goru stepped forward and grasped the knife, the gypsies cheering with approval at his move.

Goru ran his fingers over the knife's edge and tested it lovingly. The expression on his face made Mrs. Pollifax shiver. She looked up into the stolid faces of the gypsies and then at the triumphant smile on Dr. Belleaux's lips and she experienced the first chill of doubt. She realized that she had allowed herself to be tied up again, and that she was helpless. She remembered the money taken from her by the gypsy youths . . . it was so very *much* money. Now that Magda had been returned to the gypsies of what value really was she, or Colin, or his uncle or Sandor, compared to the wealth they had brought into the camp? It was wealth that would have to be given back if the gypsies chose to save them. She had trusted Anyeta but the woman was an invalid—had she really any influence? What if Goru chose to disbelieve or to ignore her? For the first time she realized that her being persuaded back to the tree could be a cunning trick, and she a fool to have trusted the persuaders.

Goru suddenly laughed and called out to one of his companions, who brought him a small jug. *"Icki,"* Goru said to Dr. Belleaux, and held out the jug to him. Dr. Belleaux sighed with exasperation as he accepted it. Another gypsy handed jugs to Stefan and to Assim, and at once jugs blossomed everywhere among the gypsies. Apparently a toast had been proposed by Goru—a toast to their murders, wondered Mrs. Pollifax?

"I don't like this," Colin said in a low voice.

Obviously Dr. Belleaux did not like it, either. Impatiently he lifted the jug to his lips, drained it, threw the empty vessel to the ground and spoke sharply to Goru. Goru, sipping his drink like a connoisseur, smiled back at him and smacked his lips appreciatively.

Angrily Dr. Belleaux seized the knife from Goru's hand. *"Budala,"* he snarled and turned to Mrs. Pollifax. "Enough delay!" he said, and looking down at her in a cold fury, he lifted the knife for its thrust into her heart.

Behind him no one stirred. The gypsies watched with a passive, detached interest, and Mrs. Pollifax realized they were not going to stop her murder. Dr. Belleaux's livid face came close and she gasped, bracing herself against his blow, and then she gasped again as he continued a headlong descent and pitched into her lap, the knife still in his hand, his body limp. He twitched once, and then was still.

"They will sleep for eight hours, they are not dead," Anyeta was explaining to Colin and Mrs. Pollifax. "We would be fools to kill a *gorgio*, the police are our enemies everywhere, like fleas forever on our backs."

An unbelievable amount of activity was taking place in the gypsy camp; Anyeta had been carried from her tent to a wagon where she sat on a cushion giving orders in a low husky voice. Her tent had been struck and packed away, and the two campfires extinguished and raked. Horses were being harnessed to the wagons, and the three casualties of the night—Magda, Sandor and Ramsey—had already been stowed carefully away in one of the wagons, wrapped in blankets and still unconscious.

"We have our own drugs, but kinder than theirs because they are herbs as old as time," she explained with a flash of a smile. "The three men will sleep dreamlessly for eight hours, and wake up refreshed. By then we must be far away."

"But where did your men carry them?" asked Colin.

"To the plane, where they have been strapped into the seats. They will make a peaceful picture when they are found. Now it is time to ask you an important question: You have found us, and you have found Magda's grandson, and soon she will open her eyes to see him, too. What do you plan to do with her?"

Mrs. Pollifax explained their hopes that Magda might be alert enough to be placed on the Friday plane at Kayseri.

"She has passport?"

"She has passport, ticket, money and clothes."

Anyeta smiled broadly. "Not money." She shook her head. "Yule!"

The youth who had robbed Mrs. Pollifax ran over, and Anyeta held out her palm. The young man grinned handsomely, brought the wad of bills from his pocket and bowed as he placed them in Anyeta's hand.

"He is very skillful, we are proud of him," Anyeta told Mrs. Pollifax. "But of course we do not steal from friends. Count it." She affectionately boxed his ears and he ran off to help with the loading. "So. You wish to take Magda to Kayseri. That is good—we head in that direction. What is more difficult is a place to hide for a day or two. You say Friday?"

"Yes. It must be Thursday by now. The plane leaves Friday morning at eight. The next plane is Monday, but who knows what could have happened by then?"

Anyeta nodded. "No hiding place is safe for that long! A place for us all to wait safely, then, during the daylight hours today. Yes I know of one, but far—we must go straight as the eagle flies toward the rock country near Ürgüp. From there it will take only hours to walk or ride to Kayseri, and it will be dark again when the time comes to get her to the airport." She nodded. "Very good."

A long shrill whistle broke the silence. "We are ready to go," Anyeta said. "We go cross-country, avoiding all roads."

Mrs. Pollifax took leave of her and hurried to the wagon in which her friends lay. Colin climbed into the van—he was to drive it a few miles from the scene and leave it hidden, to be found later. The wagons formed a line. From the lead wagon in which Anyeta and Goru rode there came a shout, and six wagons began to move into the night with only the stars to guide them south.

There was no tarpaulin over the wagon in which Mrs. Pollifax rode, and she could feel the softness of the cool night air on her cheeks. The wagon creaked and groaned over the untilled, rocky ground but the movement and the creaks were not unpleasant, and as her eyes adapted to the darkness Mrs. Pollifax could decipher rocks and boulders to left and right, and at last the silhouettes of her companions. Magda was beginning to stir at last, to fling out a hand and murmur occasional unintelligible words. The silhouette of dark curly hair beside her was Dmitri—her grandson, Mrs. Pollifax repeated to herself, still touched and amazed by the discovery. Colin drove the van that whined in low gear behind them while his uncle snored peacefully on the floor of the wagon, sharing a blanket with Sandor, who had also slipped into the exhausted sleep that still eluded Mrs. Pollifax.

Magda called out sharply, and Mrs. Pollifax crawled over Sandor and Ramsey to look at her. Dmitri was leaning over speaking to her, and Magda said, "It's you? It's really you, Dmitri?" in a wondering and astonished voice.

"Good morning," said Mrs. Pollifax. "I believe it's morning!"

Magda began to laugh. "And you too? No no, it is too much," she gasped, and reached for Mrs. Pollifax's hand. "Again you have rescued me. And found Dmitri!"

"It's been a long night," admitted Mrs. Pollifax, "but I had a great deal of help: Colin and Sandor, Colin's uncle, a girl named Sabahat and your gypsies."

Magda's laughter abruptly turned into tears, and then into exhausted, wrenching sobs.

"It's all right, Dmitri, let her cry," Mrs. Pollifax told the boy, patting his shoulder. "She'll feel better for it, she's been through so much."

Gradually Magda's tears subsided and she slept. She would need that sleep if she was to gain enough strength to board a plane within twenty-four hours—and that, thought Mrs. Pollifax as she crawled back to her corner of the wagon, was the one thing that mattered now. The seriousness of her own plight had dimmed once she had met Dmitri—and then the boy had pulled the Evil Eye from under his ragged shirt to show her, and Mrs. Pollifax had understood that she was of no importance at all to Dr. Belleaux, nor was Magda or her grandson. From the beginning he had been set upon recovering something more. What had Carstairs said? "The mystery is why Ferenci-Sabo's abductors didn't silence her on the spot by killing her—they certainly had no difficulties in gaining access to the consulate, damn it. Obviously Ferenci-Sabo still has more value to them alive."

But not because of Dmitri, Mrs. Pollifax realized. The kidnapped son of a high Bulgarian official would never bring about such a merciless pursuit. At most it would beget inquiries and protests at a government level, but not murder after murder, and certainly not the possible loss of Dr. Belleaux as a highly placed counteragent in Istanbul. Since Magda had not been killed following her abduction it was obvious that the knowledge Magda carried in her head was of less concern to the Communists than what she had carried out with her that was concrete, graspable, returnable and of an almost hysterical significance to them. Only after this had been recovered would Magda be silenced.

"A great deal changed with the invasion of Czechoslovakia," mused Mrs. Pollifax. "Perhaps even Russia's leadership changed, but certainly to the western world she turned suddenly irrational, paranoiac, unpredictable. As to what might be sealed inside that innocent-looking blue stone I can only guess, of course. What might it be to prove so threatening to the Communists? Transcripts of a terribly secret conversation? a photostatic copy of the minutes of a Politburo meeting? It would have to be an important clue as to what happened that August, and what can be expected in the future, and this would matter a great deal to NATO, to Yugoslavia and Rumania, to future nuclear pacts, to the balance of power."

Magda and her blue stone had to be gotten out of Turkey. Not even Dmitri could be involved in the departure now. Perhaps Colin could look after the child until he had acquired the necessary papers to travel. She had no illusions as to what lay in store for herself, and jail would be no place for the boy.

The caravan halted, and Goru went to the rear of the line and spoke to Colin; the van was directed off the road, and several minutes later Colin jumped into the wagon beside Mrs. Pollifax carrying the van's battery in his arms. "Good lord what terrain!" he gasped. "Thought I'd have to abandon her long before this! No wonder roads are called the life-lines of civilization."

"Where did you leave the van?" asked Mrs. Pollifax curiously.

"There's a deserted village in there—Anatolia is pock-marked with them. A well runs dry, the people just move on and start a new village. I rammed the truck into one of the buildings that still has a roof." He glanced up at the sky. "It's just past three now, you know, it'll be dawn in an hour or so, and there's that damn helicopter to worry about as soon as it's light."

"Yes, the helicopter," sighed Mrs. Pollifax.

They dozed uncomfortably for another hour. Just as the country around them was growing visible in the cold first-light they crossed a main road, the first Mrs. Pollifax had seen since they left Yozgat. They crossed it wagon by wagon, with Goru waving each one on or back. Then they resumed their interminable procession southward. It must have been the Kayseri-Kirsehir road, Colin said drowsily, but Mrs. Pollifax only half-heard him.

When she opened her eyes again Magda was awake, propped up against the side of the wagon with one hand resting on Dmitri, who had fallen asleep with his head in her lap. The sun was rising with an explosion of colors that swept the sky like a wash of watercolor. Mrs. Pollifax looked at Magda and saw that her eyes were fastened almost hypnotically on Colin's sleeping uncle. Seeing Mrs. Pollifax sit up Magda lifted her free hand and waved at her, but it was with a puzzled frown that she said, "This man here—I do not understand where he came from."

"He—just arrived," said Mrs. Pollifax with humor.

"He so much resembles someone I once knew."

"He does?"

Magda nodded. "Someone I've not seen in—oh, twenty-five years at least. Many times I've wondered what happened to that man—one does, you know," she said with a faint smile. "Yet I believed I'd forgotten him until I saw this man. That same beak of a nose—"

Mrs. Pollifax looked at Uncle Hu buried in his blanket and said with a twinkle, "His nose is all one *can* see of him. Who is the man he reminds you of—a good sort, I hope?"

Magda nodded. "I have loved only two men in my life. There was my first husband Philippe—they called him the rich French playboy but it was the big performance with him because he too was an agent." She looked across the tangle of sleeping bodies at Mrs. Pollifax. "You understand he worked for his government—the French—in Intelligence. We had one year together before he was murdered."

"By whom?" asked Mrs. Pollifax.

"They were called Reds then," said Magda. "Only they did not just murder him, they arranged it to appear I had done their work. He was shot with my small pistol, still with my fingerprints on it, and there had been arranged false evidence of a lover." She shrugged. "It was blackmail. I would have preferred to kill myself but I was expecting a child, which revived my interest in living. And they did not know I already worked for my husband's people. I took my problem to French Intelligence."

"So that's when you became a double agent."

"Yes." Magda was silent, and then, "At least until World War Two when I work also with America and England." Her lips curved ruefully. "One does not expect to love a second time. I did not believe I had the heart left."

"But you did?" suggested Mrs. Pollifax with interest.

Magda sighed. "One cannot control such matters, eh? It was only an encounter, a passing thing, it was all it could mean with me because by then I was vulnerable, my daughter a hostage growing up in Russia." She frowned. "I have learned that one's life assumes a pattern—call it karma if you will. At every turning point in my life I am always thrust back into this work, as if a firm hand insists upon it. It has not been my karma to be either wife or mother for long."

Mrs. Pollifax said, "Perhaps it is now. As I understand karma—and the subject has interested me lately—a person can eventually work through to another level, isn't this true? There are karmic debts to be paid, but if one manages them well, and cheerfully, there comes a time when one moves on to a new level, a new beginning, a different karma."

"You speak as if you feel this," said Magda curiously.

Mrs. Pollifax laughed. "I can only tell you that suddenly—after quiet years of marriage and family life, and at my age, too!—I have entered a very dangerous profession. It's preposterous, as if the page of a book had been abruptly turned over by the wind. Mistake? Coincidence? Accident? There feels more to it than that. Perhaps I enter your kind of life just as you leave it for something else now."

"I could hope this for me," said Magda soberly.

"Do keep hoping," said Mrs. Pollifax, her gaze falling on Hu Ramsey with humor and a touch of mischief. She thought that just when life appeared to have no discernible pattern there could arrive a coincidence so startling that one could envision Forces tugging, arranging, balancing, contriving and contracting all the arrivals and departures of life. Magda and Colin's uncle had met once, years ago: now they met again through the most absurd of coincidences in the center of Turkish Anatolia. Mrs. Pollifax chuckled; it was so statistically impossible that she thought it had to be an act of cosmic humor, even of cosmic playfulness.

It was growing dangerously light when a shout came from a wagon up ahead. Goru stood up and waved, pointed, and Mrs. Pollifax understood that they were reaching their destination. She looked again at the high cliff that she had been examining from a distance for some time; now it rose sharply above them on their right, appearing to almost touch the sky. Here and there holes had been punched through the cliff by a giant hand, like a great wall with windows in it. Mrs. Pollifax sat up, alert and interested.

In the rubble that spilled down from the cliff like lava she could make out the shapes of crumbling houses; the hill running up to the cliff was honeycombed with caves, holes and the ruins of abandoned buildings. The wagons ahead had already begun to turn and head up the hill through the debris in a circling, ascending line. "What a wonderful hiding place!" said Mrs. Pollifax. "Unless—" She paused doubtfully. "Unless it's so good that it becomes the first place Dr. Belleaux looks for us."

Colin shook his head. "Not the first. I've driven through this part of the country with Uncle Hu, and it's even more dramatic further along. The rocks fairly jump out of the earth like weird stalactites. At Göreme they're called fairy tale chimneys—the early Christians hid in those rock chimneys centuries ago, hollowing them out inside and carving air holes and windows. They left behind fantastic Byzantine frescoes on their interior walls. The whole valley is full of surprises."

"Really? I wish I'd pinned the guidebook to my trousers."

"You ran out of pins," Colin reminded her.

The first wagon had reached the summit, and Goru had climbed out, looking small and doll-like against the great height of the wall behind him, and separated from the rest of them by the mountain of rubble. Their own wagon was lurching and slipping now as it followed the narrow rock-strewn path upward toward the top. Mrs. Pollifax clung to the sides of the wagon and prayed. Each time she looked ahead, a wagon in the line ahead had disappeared and she could only hope that it had safely reached Goru and been directed out of sight, and had not instead plunged into a hole or rolled back down the hill. They climbed higher and higher until Goru came into sight, suddenly his own size again. They had reached the top of the rubble, with the cliff above them.

By a curious freak of nature there was no rubble close to the cliff wall, and a kind of primitive, washed-out road curved up and down behind the houses that had once been built into the hill and inhabited. But as the wall had eroded over the decades—perhaps even centuries—the rocks and silt it sent down had fallen upon the houses, missing the small avenue directly under the wall, but leaving holes in the roofs that it did not completely demolish, and piling debris around the sinking homes. Along this primitive avenue the wagons had stopped, each in front of a ruin that still boasted a roof or half-roof while the men dug out rocks to allow their wagons inside. One by one Mrs. Pollifax saw the wagons backed out of view.

Their driver was Yule, who leaped down and began shouldering aside rocks—they were now the only wagon ex-

posed. Colin jumped down to help, and behind her Mrs. Pollifax heard a startled voice say, "Wotthehell!"

"Sandor," she murmured, smiling, and turned.

Sandor was sitting erect rubbing his head but his eyes
were on Magda and Ramsey. Mrs. Pollifax saw that these
two were both awake and staring at each other with interest
and astonishment; she had the impression that they must
have been mutely observing one another for some time.

Colin's uncle said abruptly, "You're thinner. You never did
care sufficiently about meals—no schedule at all. If you'd
married me I should have insisted upon your eating. Why
didn't you?"

"Why didn't I which—marry you, or eat?"

"You should have done both, you know. I've felt damnably
juvenile not marrying all these years, but there's simply
been no one to equal you. Why didn't you marry me?"

"I had a daughter in Russia."

"You could have told me, couldn't you?"

"Never," she said fondly. "You know you would have
charged the Kremlin, Hugh, demanding she be brought to
England—you would have gotten your head chopped off."

"It's France that has the guillotine, in Moscow I think it
would be a firing squad," he reminded her.

Sandor was grinning broadly. He climbed past them to
Mrs. Pollifax. "She knows him too!" he said.

At that moment someone shouted, and Goru came running toward them looking visibly alarmed. Ramsey spoke to
him in Turkish and looked appalled. "It's the plane!" he
shouted. "Get the wagon hidden! There's a plane on the
horizon heading this way!"

CHAPTER 17

TWO MEN APPEARED FROM NOWHERE AND TOOK away the horse. Five more men raced from a hole in the rocks and actually lifted the wagon over a wall of tumbling stone and into the cellar of a house. The wagon sustained only one casualty—a wheel fell off—but the miracle was that it had not happened sooner.

Their hiding place was not unpleasant. The brilliant morning sun fell through the half-ruined floor in lattice-work squares and stripes. There were stone walls on three sides of them, and half a roof over their heads but the front of the house had long since vanished, and from the shadows Mrs. Pollifax had a breathtaking panoramic view across the valley. It was like hiding under a porch that had been swept to the top of a mountain.

From here Mrs. Pollifax could see the helicopter move slowly across the valley in the tilting, gliding, oddly tipsy fashion that to Mrs. Pollifax confounded all laws of air flight. It drew nearer, disappeared behind the cliff and then suddenly roared down over their heads. For a full moment it hung suspended over them, a giant eye searching for one tell-tale slip, one unexplained shadow, one sign of careless movement. It was frightening. When it lifted and began to beat its way slowly down to the other end of the cliff Mrs. Pollifax realized that she had been holding her breath. She expelled it slowly, realizing that this could happen again and again during the day. It was not a happy thought.

Magda said suddenly, angrily, "I cannot take a plane tomorrow morning and leave Dmitri to this. Never."

Mrs. Pollifax turned and looked into her face. The helicopter had affected her in the same way, delivering them all into a nightmare inhabited by birds of prey that swept down from the sky to look for them. "Yes, it's time to make plans," she said firmly. "Let's go and find Anyeta. The plane is gone?"

Colin nodded. "It disappeared southward."

"Good. We'll talk."

They formed a circle inside the cave in which Anyeta had taken refuge. "We move at dark," Anyeta said. "Goru says that will be about nine-thirty tonight. It will be necessary to move slowly in order to be careful, and because the way is not familiar. Goru does not know where the aerodrome is at Kayseri."

"I do," said Hu Ramsey. "Fortunately it's to the west of the town—on this side of it—so that there's no need to go through Kayseri. Look here, if I went back and got the van—"

"I used up nearly all of the spare gas last night," said Colin. "I'd calculate about ten more miles of gas are left in the tank. Twelve at most."

"Damn," said Uncle Hu mildly. "Colin, you know how far away the van is. Where would the nearest petrol station be?"

"Nearest to the van, you mean? Kirsehir definitely. But if you're thinking of retrieving it to get Magda to the aerodrome then you've got to remember that the search for the van may not have been called off yet. The license may still be on their lists. Someone's bound to stop you again, as they did at Yozgat, and that's perfectly all right if you're alone but if you ever had Magda and Mrs. Pollifax with you—" Colin shook his head. "Kaput. Finis!"

Mrs. Pollifax nodded. "He's quite right. I think Magda *must* get to the aerodrome by wagon, the van's too conspicuous."

Magda looked pensive. "I've no reservation for the eight o'clock flight, or even for the London flight. What if there is no room for me?"

Mrs. Pollifax nodded. "We must organize this very very carefully. Like generals plotting a battle."

"Gung ho and all that," suggested Colin, grinning.

"Exactly. Goru, you say you don't know where the

aerodrome is. I think someone must go and find it—now, while it's daylight."

Anyeta translated this to Goru, who replied. "He will go himself," she said. "Alone. He will take a horse and find the best route for the wagons, also."

"There's another possibility," went on Mrs. Pollifax. "Magda wants to know that Dmitri will not become involved in this. She also needs a reservation for the flight—it would certainly be reassuring to have one for Alice Dexter White clear through to London—and Mr. Ramsey has his van to retrieve, which has in it roughly enough gas to get to Kirsehir." She lifted her gaze. "Mr. Ramsey, if you could take Dmitri with you and reach that van sometime today, then you could drive it to Kirsehir for gas, and telephone the airport in Kayseri for Magda's flight reservations. You could also provide a—well, a diversion. Kirsehir looks quite removed from Kayseri on this map. If the police should stop the van you'd have with you only a small boy picked up on the road. You've already been checked out at Yozgat—it's possible you wouldn't be taken to jail again. You could then drive on to Ankara."

Ramsey shot her a quick glance. "Quite right, of course." He looked distinctly unhappy but it was to his credit, thought Mrs. Pollifax, that he did not protest leaving Magda. He was a man who could accept necessity.

"You would do that?" Magda said hopefully. "Hugh, I cannot tell you how grateful I would be."

"Of course I can do it," he said crisply. "Dmitri, you'll try me out next as a companion?"

"Must?" he said in a dispirited voice to Magda.

She spoke to him gently in Russian and he listened gravely, then with growing brightness. "Da," he told Ramsey, nodding. "I go. I am—how you say—gung ho?"

"Good boy," Ramsey said, ruffling his hair.

"You will need a horse and a guide," Anyeta told him. "Yule will go—he knows where the van is hidden, and he can bring the horse back before night. Anything else?"

They all leaned over the map to pinpoint their present location, the best route to Kirsehir for Ramsey, and the precise area of the Kayseri aerodrome. "Don't head south," Uncle Hu warned Goru. "The police have a station here"—he pointed— "at Inescu. As you can see, that's a little too near for comfort."

Goru nodded and stood up. *"Allaha ismarladik,"* he said.

"Gule, gule," said Uncle Hu, shaking his hand.

Mrs. Pollifax was busy thinking. "Magda will need sleep and food today," she told Anyeta. "Near the end of the day I'll fit her into my American clothes, which she can wear under her Turkish ones." Was there anything else, she wondered, mentally ticking off the plans. Magda would still be very weak. If they could reach the airport while it was still dark a wagon could deposit Magda very near to the air terminal without such unconventional arrival being noticed; she could peel off her Turkish clothes, leave them behind in the wagon and walk into the terminal as Alice Dexter White, American tourist. If her reservation had already been made by telephone then she need only pay for it—automatically Mrs. Pollifax felt for the wad of money pinned to her baggy pants and nodded—and then walk through Customs to the lounge.

"A suitcase," said Mrs. Pollifax. "She ought to have a suitcase like everyone else."

"Good thinking," said Colin, "but we've only that horrible cardboard thing Madrali fetched us. An American tourist carrying *that would* be frighteningly conspicuous."

Uncle Hu said, "Wait a minute, I can contribute one from the van—Yule can bring it back with him tonight. It's old and battered, I've kept film in it for years but it's definitely Bond Street and very British."

"Then that's it, isn't it?" announced Colin.

Anyeta produced a pair of crutches and joined them as they walked outside to see the horses saddled. Goru was just leaving, and she called out to him; he nodded and waved. "I told him to make his way to the end of the cliff, following the shade, so that if the plane should come back and see him there would be no sign of where he came from. You must do the same, Mr. Ramsey."

He nodded absently and turned to Magda. "You will be careful," he said flatly.

"I will be careful."

"It's not easy to leave you when I've just found you. You'll wait for me and Dmitri in Scotland?"

She nodded.

He leaned over and held her for a moment silently, and

then he turned to Dmitri, smiled and said, "Well, Dmitri? We begin a long journey, you and I."

For a moment Dmitri and Magda clung to each other, and then he carefully removed the Evil Eye from around his neck and passed it over his grandmother's head. "Now is yours to guard," he said.

One of the men stationed above them on the cliffside shouted words down to Anyeta. "He says there is no sign of the plane, it is time you go quickly."

Lifting Dmitri to the saddle of his horse Ramsey said firmly, "We mustn't keep Yule waiting. Off we go, Dmitri. Gung ho, what?"

When they had disappeared along the cliff Mrs. Pollifax and Colin lingered outside to look out over the bright, sunlit, dusty valley. "Tomorrow at this time," began Mrs. Pollifax, seating herself on a crumbling wall.

"Yes?" said Colin, joining her.

She shook her head. "It's what makes sleep so impossible— the waiting," Mrs. Pollifax explained. "The not-knowing." She stared across the valley, her eyes narrowed against the brilliance of sun on whitened rock. "I love this part of the country," she said suddenly. "I've never seen anything quite like it. I had thought Turkey so dark—"

"Its history is dark."

"But look at it—everything sun-baked, the color of cream and old lace and ripe wheat and bleached rock and yellow grass, and then this brilliant blue sky and every now and then clumps of green the color of jade. I do wish I were an artist. What on earth are you scribbling?"

Colin grinned. "I intend to spend this endless day of ours shooting film, and I'm jotting down your adjectives. Uncle Hu could use them. He does his own narrations, you know."

"Would I get residuals?" asked Mrs. Pollifax with interest.

"Would you insist on it?"

"No."

"Good," said Colin briskly, "because I'm sure Uncle Hu doesn't even know what the word means, and the most you could expect would be a thank-you note."

He added firmly, with a confidence she'd not heard before, "I've decided there's something I can do to pay Uncle

Hu back for his kindnesses, and that's to film the gypsies. You may not realize it, but in all his years in this country he's never been able to catch more than a passing shot of them from his car." He added dryly, "You can perhaps understand the difficulties in approaching them now. It's bothered him excessively. Now at last he has the opportunity to spend a day with them, film them, make friends with them, and damned if he's not off on an errand of mercy. The chance of a lifetime and he's missing it! I'm going to ask Anyeta if I can poke around filming her gypsies today."

"I'll come with you," said Mrs. Pollifax.

The hours of the day were long but not unpleasant. In midmorning they ate warmed-over *domatesli pilaf* heated by Anyeta on a small, almost smokeless charcoal brazier. The horses were fed. Sandor took over the mending of the damaged wagon wheel and Colin roamed ubiquitously over the cliff with his camera, popping in and out of caves and cellars, following Magda and Mrs. Pollifax to the well when they drew water for Anyeta, filming the gypsy children at their play and the women at work.

The helicopter did not return but twice a small plane flew over, sending everyone into hiding until it was gone. "Police, I think," said Colin, squinting up at it through holes in the roof, and Anyeta sent out orders to double the lookouts posted on the cliff.

"She is a queen, you know—literally," Magda said during a moment when Anyeta ventured out on crutches to oversee the wagon's mending. "It is she who holds all the people together. Not only these, but many more."

"Queen of gypsies!" mused Mrs. Pollifax. "And now I have met one personally . . . She comes from Bulgaria?"

"Oh no," Magda said firmly. "No, I am not the only person she smuggled out. The gypsies in Bulgaria—it is a country very close to Russia ideologically—are being absorbed into Bulgarian life. They allow no nonsense, the Bulgars, and the gypsy children are made to go to school, to conform, to put aside their heritage and become good workers in the Bulgarian Communist life. It troubles the older ones. No, Anyeta and Goru also smuggled out illegally some of the Rom who wished to leave. Not many but a few."

"Not all of the eastern European countries are so rigid then?" asked Mrs. Pollifax.

"Oh no! Anyeta's roots are in Rumania, and from Rumania the gypsies wander freely into Yugoslavia over the mountains, and from there into Italy or western Germany."

"How did she lose the use of her legs—polio?" asked Mrs. Pollifax.

Magda laughed. "That is something not even I can discover! But it is said by the Rom that her gift for clairvoyance tripled when she lost the power to walk—as if all her strength went to this gift for the psychic." She shook her head admiringly. "She is an astonishing woman. When I first met her—"

"Where?" asked Mrs. Pollifax eagerly.

"It was in Budapest many years ago, in a cafe, and she was wearing pearls and diamonds. I was stunned to learn she was an Inglescu." Magda looked at Mrs. Pollifax and nodded. "Is this not amazing? Can you see her in diamonds? It is the wonder of life, such things. Perhaps you have heard of _____?" She mentioned the name of a European concert violinist.

"Indeed I have," said Mrs. Pollifax. "I heard him play years ago in Carnegie Hall on one of his few American tours."

Magda nodded. "He was half-gypsy, you know. That was Anyeta's husband. But she is *all* gypsy, and grew sick from the *gorgio*'s life. I hear that she became very thin, very pale, very sad, and nearly died. She had to come back to her people."

"To this," said Mrs. Pollifax reflectively, looking out at the sun and the white rocks. "I can only barely understand. Two days ago I wouldn't have understood at all."

Magda said softly, "The gypsies have a song—the words go like this:

> Worldly goods that possess,
> Own and destroy you.
> Love must be like the blowing wind.
> Capture the wind between walls
> and it becomes stale.
> Open tents.

Open hearts.
Let the wind blow . . ."

They were silent and then Mrs. Pollifax nodded. "Yes," she said quietly.

Magda slept, and seeing Anyeta watch her Mrs. Pollifax said curiously, "Does your gift for clairvoyance tell you anything?"

Anyeta was silent and then she said reluctantly, "I get no picture of Magda on a plane. Something is in the way, something intrudes. I am uneasy . . ."

Night came swiftly, like a blanket tossed over the plateau abruptly snuffing out the twilight. Yule had returned leading the spare horse. Yes, the Englishman and Dmitri had reached the van in midafternoon and he had watched while the battery was put in and he had seen the van leave. Its dust had been visible for some miles, and he was sure the two had reached the Kirsehir road successfully. Goru did not get back until dark; he had seen many police patroling the roads but he had avoided them and discovered the aerodrome. He had also found a valley through the mountains that would take them through the rock country without crossing any major roads. He looked exhausted, and Mrs. Pollifax guessed that he had combed the whole valley for the best route. He would have made a wonderful general, she thought, glad that he was on their side, but of course he was already Anyeta's guerrilla chieftain as he moved the gypsies over borders and through hostile countries. She watched him touch Magda on the shoulder and smile at her, and she realized the many years these people had known Magda, building a relationship that was tolerant and free and fiercely loyal.

Under her Turkish baggy pants Magda wore Mrs. Pollifax's knit suit and blouse. Now Mrs. Pollifax gave her passport and money. "In case we are separated," she said, trying not to remember Anyeta's uneasiness.

They moved out a little after ten o'clock. There had been some discussion of three wagons heading south to divert attention, but this had been quickly vetoed. Anyeta said flatly, "We Zingari stick together. We live, breathe, eat, die together. We also fight together." Mrs. Pollifax was inclined to

be grateful for this. It was true that six wagons made more
noise, were less mobile and more conspicuous but she too
felt more secure with a full complement of gypsies around
her. They were a formidable group to defy, as she knew personally from the previous evening.

They bypassed the town of Ürgüp and moved across the
valley into the shadows of *Topuz Dagi* that unyieldingly
guarded the eastern perimeter, its peak remote and sharp
against the stars. The sky was brighter tonight. "There'll be
a moon later," Colin said. "It must already be rising behind
that mountain range."

"How far is it to Kayseri in miles?" asked Mrs. Pollifax.

He shook his head. "Too far for wagons moving this
slowly, but perhaps Goru plans to camp at some point along
the way and continue on horseback. Or perhaps this is a
shortcut. It's hard to tell by the map."

Magda said firmly, "Trust Goru. He fought with Yugoslav
partisans during the second world war, he can be very cunning." She turned to Mrs. Pollifax with a shy smile. "You
have already trusted me—you have not asked why I go to
Scotland. If I get away."

Mrs. Pollifax laughed softly. "But I knew you would explain if you chose to!"

Magda nodded. "Hugh has a hunting lodge there. If I
succeed in getting to London I will send one cable to Washington from the airport and then I shall disappear again. You
understand I shall be very stubborn until Dmitri is allowed
to join me."

Mrs. Pollifax considered this and nodded. She supposed
that one small boy could very easily be overlooked or ignored by governments once they were satisfied, and that
even Carstairs could be rendered impotent by a government.
"A little friendly persuasion," she said, nodding. "Yes, I
understand. I won't ask for the address."

"Thank you."

The wagons jolted and bounced and creaked, it was very
like their journey the night before, the cold following a day
of heat, the same stars overhead, same sounds of muffled
voices. But the radiance of the hidden moon gave an almost
Biblical quality to the procession of primitive wagons moving across the austere, harsh countryside. The earth here was

called *tuff*, Colin said, composed of ashes and mud and rock; there were no trees, its only fruit was the rocks, and there were so many of these that at times it became necessary to climb down from the wagons and lift them over boulders.

Sometime around two o'clock the line stopped and rough bread and jugs of water were distributed while Goru walked up and down the line checking wheels and axles on the carts. No one spoke above a whisper and the line moved on again soon. It was incredible country: the moonlight picked out whole forests of needle-shaped rock, a valley of rock chimneys arising white under the moon, a cluster of cone-shaped hovels like beehives.

It was four o'clock in the morning when word swept up and down the procession that they were being followed by a man on horseback. For the first time Mrs. Pollifax realized that Goru had scouts ahead and behind them but this realization came late to reassure her. The news of a pursuer struck her as inexplicable and ominous.

"It could be Sebastien," Colin said hopefully.

"Sebastien," repeated Mrs. Pollifax, remembering Yozgat. "Yes, it could be Sebastien," she said politely.

"One person on horseback is scarcely a threat to some thirty gypsies," Colin pointed out. "Why doesn't Goru stop and find out who it is?" He jumped down. "I'll walk ahead and ask."

He was back several minutes later wearing a frown. "Whoever it is he stays behind us at some distance. It was thought a coincidence at first—someone's trail crossing ours—but the rider takes the same turns, the same trails. Goru says there isn't time to stop, it's half-past four and the important thing is getting Magda to the aerodrome before eight."

"Quite so," Mrs. Pollifax said with feeling.

But uneasiness permeated the caravan. The line moved faster, and when a wagon needed help over the rocks there were sharp words exchanged. Yet whoever followed showed no sign of moving closer to them. Nothing changed except the sky, which was whitening with dawn, and the terrain which grew flatter as the rocks thinned. They were leaving the volcanic country behind them and returning to the flat and dusty Anatolian plateau. Somewhere on this plateau, between them and the foothills of the high mountains in the distance, lay Kayseri and the airport.

"How far now?" asked Mrs. Pollifax of Colin.

"I don't know," he said shortly.

"Then what time is it?"

"A few minutes after five."

As he said this Goru lifted his hand and called out a sharp command from the front, the sound of his voice startling after so many hours of caution. In the east the sky had turned into mother-of-pearl and the tip of an orange sun was lifting itself over the peak of the mountains. Goru was waving them to a halt because two men on horseback were approaching them from the north.

"They're in uniform," Mrs. Pollifax said as they drew closer, not hurrying but keeping their horses to a steady walk.

"The constabulary," Colin said shortly. "Rural police."

"Oh," said Mrs. Pollifax.

The two men rode up to Goru, their faces not unfriendly. They looked pleasant, relaxed, two men on normal patrol. For a few minutes they exchanged words with Goru and then, while one man continued idly conversing, the other rode slowly up and down the wagon line looking into the faces of the gypsies and glancing over and into the wagons. He rode back and the three-way conversation continued endlessly. Goru nodded and stood up, calling out to the gypsies.

Casually Sandor strolled back to them from Anyeta's wagon in which he was riding. He said, "They wish to see all identity cards."

"But this is going to take a long time!" said Mrs. Pollifax despairingly.

"Yes."

"Why the devil can't we just tie them up and take them along?" asked Colin irritably. "I still have Stefan's pistol!"

Sandor grinned. "What a lion you are! You wish them to know we have something to hide? When a police sees gypsies he either spits and rides on, or stops to see what they have stolen today. Please, a sense of dimension!"

"I think he means perspective," Magda said with a wry smile as she handed Sandor the card of *Nimet Aziz*. Mrs. Pollifax parted with *Yurgadil* and Colin with *Nazmi*, and Sandor carried them back to the police.

There followed an interminable wait, tense with anxiety lest the police ask to question each gypsy personally and discover that three of them were frauds. The police talked on and on while one of them shuffled through the pile of thirty cards, speaking sometimes to Goru or to Anyeta, sometimes to each other. Once they laughed—"Are they telling *jokes*?" whispered Colin indignantly—and then at last the papers were handed back to Goru and the wagons were waved ahead.

But they had been stopped for more than forty-five minutes, and it was now nearly six. Mrs. Pollifax was beginning to wonder if Magda could possibly reach the aerodrome in the two hours remaining to them. Her doubts were silent but she sensed that it was a question that hung suspended over the whole caravan as it moved forward. As for the two policemen, they had ridden off at a gallop and nothing could be seen of them but a cloud of dust.

"*Now* they hurry," said Colin bitterly. "Do you think we passed inspection?"

Mrs. Pollifax said tartly, "It depends on what they were looking for. If they were looking specifically for gypsies then they found them—and also did a brilliant job of slowing us down."

They were tired, hungry and dusty now, but they were apparently nearing a more civilized area: half an hour later they skirted a small village of a dozen buildings steaming in the early morning sun and threaded their way between vineyards into bare fields again. Sandor walked back to them with a new message from Anyeta.

"Goru wishes the wagons to go two-by-two now, one beside the other. This wagon will move next to his." He translated this to Yule, and their wagon bypassed the others and drew abreast of Anyeta and Goru.

Leaning over between wagons Anyeta said, "You must stay close to Magda now." There was a mute warning in her eyes for Mrs. Pollifax. "Very close, you understand?"

Mrs. Pollifax nodded. What did Anyeta see? Of what was she afraid? But it was not only Anyeta: Goru stood up, bracing himself, and tossed a club to Yule across the wagons and followed this with a string bag that contained—of all things—perfectly round, small rocks.

And then Mrs. Pollifax understood: she too heard the helicopter. As she looked up it came darting over the swelling hill ahead of them, delicate, small, yet monstrous, like a blown-up metallic dragonfly.

"So we are to meet the good doctor again," said Colin grimly. "But he's a fool this time! What can he do against so many of us?"

Mrs. Pollifax did not reply. Dr. Belleaux might be many things but he was not a fool. She looked around her thoughtfully. Behind them lay the vineyards. Ahead, to their right, a village graveyard populated a gently sloping, treeless hill. She could see nothing, but her skin prickled uneasily.

Into this the helicopter descended, sending clouds of dust into their eyes. Mrs. Pollifax coughed and ducked her head, drawing her shawl over her nose and eyes. When she peered through a slit of the shawl she saw the helicopter resting lightly on the ground some forty yards away, its blades still whirring, its dust almost blanketing them all. "Why the devil doesn't he turn that blasted machine off!" cried Colin, jumping down. "Get under the wagon or behind it or you'll be blinded by the dust!" he shouted, and held out a hand to Magda and Mrs. Pollifax.

Goru was shouting orders. Everyone seemed to be shouting to someone else. The door of the helicopter opened and Dr. Belleaux and Stefan jumped down with pistols. From somewhere on the right a gun was fired—it came from the graveyard on the hill, realized Mrs. Pollifax—and now she understood Dr. Belleaux's confidence: he had not come alone, he had at last joined forces with the Turkish police.

"Mon dieu!" cried Magda as the graveyard came to life and the police began pouring down the hill.

But they were still some distance away, and Mrs. Pollifax realized why Dr. Belleaux had left the engine alive on the helicopter: he had arrived but he was facing the gypsies for these few minutes with only his gun and Stefan's. She saw his uneasiness, his uncertainty, his determination to remain just beside the door of the helicopter lest a quick retreat prove necessary. Goru too, saw this and suddenly appeared from behind the plane. With a club he knocked the gun from Dr. Belleaux's hand.

Stefan whirled on him but at once other gypsies swept forward to surround them. Yule was knocked flat—Stefan was not an incompetent bodyguard—and a club flew into the air.

"To the vineyard! Hide in the vineyard!" shouted Anyeta from her wagon. "Quickly!"

"She's right—hurry!" cried Colin, tugging at her arm.

But Mrs. Pollifax shook her head. There was no future for them hiding in a vineyard, and the police had broken into a run as they crossed the fields. They would be here in a minute or two—three at the most—and it would be the finish for them. Magda would never reach the aerodrome, or her eight o'clock plane to freedom. Instead she was staring at the helicopter, momentarily abandoned and unguarded. It was a small miracle: how often did miracles such as this occur? She said, "Colin, can you fly a helicopter?"

He gaped at her. "God no!"

Magda threw back her head and laughed. "Mrs. Pollifax, you are irrepressible! Do you really think—"

"There's no other way," Mrs. Pollifax said firmly, and began to run, dragging Magda with her.

Colin hesitated, looked helplessly around him, then at the two fleeing women, and followed. Together they ran at break-neck speed around and through the melee of fist-fighters to reach the door of the helicopter. Mrs. Pollifax boosted Magda inside, pulled herself up and turned to give Colin a hand. At the same moment they were seen by the approaching police. A shot was fired and Colin fell back.

"Go!" he shouted. "Go!"

"Of course not!" cried Mrs. Pollifax, still clinging to his hand, and dragged him bodily over the threshold. "Bolt the doors!" she told Magda. "Keep everybody out!"

"But can you drive a helicopter?" asked Magda, leaning across Colin and bolting the doors.

Mrs. Pollifax snapped, "Of course not!" and sat down and looked at the levers. There were two of them, one jutting straight up from the floor, the other running parallel to her leg from behind the seat. She grasped the latter, closed her eyes, said a prayer, and pulled. The helicopter gave a little jump—they were still alive. Heartened, she grasped the second lever and thrust it forward and they hovered several feet from the ground, going nowhere but considerably frightening the people around the plane, who began to scatter. Mrs.

Pollifax tackled the levers more sternly, and with a leap they began moving sideways, threatening to level gypsies as well as police. "Courage, Emily," she told herself, and returned to the first lever—and suddenly they were sailing over the heads of the gypsies and the police. "Well!" she gasped, and drew a breath of satisfaction. "Well!" she said, and only wished she could remember what she had done.

"Good God we're up," said Colin weakly.

"Be still, it's bloody but only a flesh wound," Magda told him. "Lie down!"

"Lie down?" Colin said. "Lie down when I've survived being shot only to be abducted in a helicopter flown by a madwoman? Mrs. Pollifax—"

"Ssh," she told him sternly. "Ssh—I'm driving this thing. Now where's the airport?" They were flying at low-level—in jumps, rather like a kangaroo—while Mrs. Pollifax tested levers, trying to find out which took them up, and which forward and sideways.

"Look out!" screamed Magda as they narrowly averted a tree.

The helicopter leaped, dropped, skimmed across a field almost on its side, turned, lifted and settled at a more conservative altitude. "I wish you would speak more quietly," Mrs. Pollifax said reprovingly. "When you shout in my ear I jump and so does my hand and so does the plane."

"Look—there's a highway!" Magda gasped, kneeling behind Mrs. Pollifax.

"Good—we'll follow it," said Mrs. Pollifax. "Colin, what time is it?"

He braced an arm, lifted it and scowled at his watch. "Seven-fifteen."

Magda said, "You're too low, Mrs. Pollifax, we're going to hit the cars." Forgetting to be quiet she screamed, "Look out!"

The plane jumped. Cars scattered to left and to right. Mrs. Pollifax tugged at the first lever that met her hand and they zoomed heavenward. Shakily she said, "We badly need an airport."

"I'm looking, believe me," said Magda.

They flew over Kayseri—it had to be Kayseri—and barely missed the top of a minaret that rose like a needle in their path. "Up!" screamed Magda.

"They build them too high!" shouted Mrs. Pollifax peevishly, pulled the wrong lever and sent them moving crab-like back to the minaret. Furiously she tugged at another lever and they went skyward again.

"I see the airport!" cried Magda triumphantly, and there it was, a gloriously clear space a mile or two away decorated with runways and a control tower. "Watch those buildings!" Magda cried despairingly. "We're hovering!"

"I know we're hovering," cried Mrs. Pollifax, "but I can't seem to—" They shot abruptly forward, dropped low, then suddenly lower, the motor died and they came to rest on the ground. "I think we just ran out of gas," said Mrs. Pollifax. "Where are we?"

Magda said calmly, "We've just landed in the middle of Kayseri's public square, and barely missed a policeman directing traffic."

Mrs. Pollifax nodded and opened her eyes. "Yes, I see him," she said with a sigh. "A great many people seem to be looking at us, too."

From the floor of the helicopter Colin said, "Then get moving! Run! Grab a taxi! Leave the rest to me!"

He was quite right, of course. Mrs. Pollifax opened the door next to her, which was happily furthest from the policeman, slid out, extended a hand to Magda and they jumped down. For just a moment they stood hand in hand, blinking a little at the gathering crowd, then with pleasant nods and smiles they made their way to the sidewalk, allowed the crowd to stream past them, and casually slipped down a side street to look for a taxi.

"Head for the ladies room," Mrs. Pollifax told Magda. "Don't wait for me—two of us might draw attention. Go in, peel off your Turkish clothes and bundle them into a wastebasket."

It was precisely 7:35 as they entered the air terminal, and as she saw Magda escape into the ladies room Mrs. Pollifax looked around her and became aware of how they must look to the civilized world following their trip across Turkey by bus, car, wagon and helicopter. She moved humbly into a corner and waited.

Ten minutes later there emerged from the ladies room a thin, erect and distinguished-looking woman with head high, eyes alert and navy knit suit only slightly askew. Mrs. Pollifax smiled approvingly. Magda walked to the flight desk and with exquisite aplomb drew out bills from the shawl she carried over one arm. Several minutes later she reached Passport Control and held out her passport with confidence. The official took it, looked deeply into Magda's face, showed it to his companion officer, stamped it and with a nod returned it.

Not until she reached the door did Magda turn, her glance sweeping the lobby. When she saw Mrs. Pollifax in her dusty baggy pants and shawl her mouth curved slightly. They exchanged a long expressionless glance and then almost imperceptibly Magda lifted one hand in a gesture that could have been a wave or a salute.

It was now 7:55. Mrs. Pollifax moved to the window and watched Magda board the plane, watched the hands of the clock tick away five minutes, saw the stairs removed, the door closed, watched the plane begin to taxi down the runway. It stopped at the beginning of the long runway. "Go, go, go," whispered Mrs. Pollifax. The plane hesitated and then began to move again. As its wheels lifted Mrs. Pollifax slowly expelled her breath, and there were tears in her eyes.

Magda was airborne.

She turned and walked the length of the terminal to the front door. She did not falter when she saw the crowds gathering there, nor flinch at sight of police hurrying inside and barking out orders to the crowd of porters and tourists. As she drew nearer one of the police looked up and saw her and stepped forward.

"Mrs. Pollifax?" he said.

She sighed and nodded. Behind him she saw Dr. Belleaux stepping out of a car. He wore a strip of adhesive across one cheek but aside from this he looked his usual cool, authoritative self.

"You are wanted for questioning in the murder of Henry Miles," he said. "Come with us, please."

CHAPTER 18

HER CELL WAS SMALL, MADE OF STONE AND VERY old but not at all picturesque or pleasant. In fact it smelled. It had been cold and damp when she entered it at half-past eight, and then as the day progressed it became damp and hot with a sticky jungle humidity. There was a jug of water in one corner of the cell but no one brought food; no one came near her at all, for any purpose whatever, and this alarmed her because she had expected to tell her story to the police at once. Now she had no idea of what was happening, or of how much damage Dr. Belleaux might be doing while she was imprisoned here. She knew that Magda's plane had safely left—she had seen this for herself—but Magda could have been intercepted at Ankara or Istanbul, and might very easily be sitting in a cell now, too. The thought of such a defeat appalled her.

The hours crawled by, each of them bringing their own hell of doubt. Was Magda still on the plane? Was she even alive? Did Dr. Belleaux possess the Evil Eye by now? The very fact that no one came to her cell made her wonder if Dr. Belleaux was not exercising a great deal of authority; it was he who could least afford her communicating with anyone in charge here.

But if only *someone* would come! It was maddening to sit here charged with such a small, sad and truthless crime when she had news so explosive, and worries so alarming.

Toward noon she began to pace her cell, staring in

165

exasperation at the tiny window high in the wall, or standing by the door in the hope of hearing footsteps outside. There was nothing. The day grew hotter and the walls of her cell began to literally sweat, the moisture running down and dropping with a soft *phfft* on the stones. Just in case her cell was wired she took to saying in a clear voice every thirty minutes, "I must talk to someone in charge, I have information for the Turkish government." No one came, no one listened, there was only heat and silence. After a number of hours Mrs. Pollifax ceased her pacing and wearily sat down on the metal bunk, feeling very depressed and extremely hungry.

She had completely lost track of time when the door to her cell suddenly opened. The light had grown dimmer—it must be late afternoon, she guessed—and it was difficult to see more than the outline of the man, who said briskly, "I am sorry, Mrs. Pollifax! There has been no time to interview you, and you have had a long wait indeed. You will come with me please to a"—she heard him sniff—"more agreeable place."

"Yes," she said in a dispirited voice.

He led her down a long, dimly lit dungeon of a corridor and up worn stairs to a more civilized hall. At an open door he turned to wait for her. "In here, please," he said. It was a beautiful door—pure mahogany—and she realized that she was being ushered into an office. It was a vast improvement. There was sunshine in the room, as well as fresh air, and much more mahogany. Only the bars across the windows reminded her that she was still in prison.

She sat down in a leather chair beside his desk and now that her eyes were becoming accustomed to the light she examined the man with some surprise. "We've met before," she said abruptly.

"Yes," he said, sitting down and smiling pleasantly at her. "In Istanbul, at Central Headquarters. I am Mr. Piskapos."

"Of course," she said, recalling the man in plainclothes who had remained beside the window, scarcely speaking. "May I ask how Mr. Ramsey is? Mr. Colin Ramsey?"

"Oh yes, the young man found in the helicopter." He nodded. "Just a flesh wound, quite negligible."

"Has he—uh—spoken with you?"

Mr. Piskapos smiled at her with interest. "Now what would he speak to me about, Mrs. Pollifax, eh?" He leaned over and flicked on the switch of a tape recorder. "Have some figs," he said, holding out to her a polished wooden bowl of fruit. "I must question you of many matters. Food will be brought you soon, but you must be very hungry."

"Thank you," she said, and accepted a fig and held it—it was a very sticky fig. She realized that after all these hours of waiting she had finally acquired someone to speak to, and she no longer had any idea of what to say. She could not think of any questions that might not provoke graver dangers for Magda—or Dmitri—or Colin and his uncle, or the gypsies, or even herself; nor of any answers that would not betray her connection with Mr. Carstairs and his organization.

"But let us get on with this," said Mr. Piskapos, and added calmly, "I am a member of the Turkish Intelligence, Mrs. Pollifax, and so you may speak frankly with me. You are an American agent, are you not?"

She shook her head. "You flatter me, Mr. Piskapos, I am an American tourist."

He nodded. "Then let us not pursue *that* detail any further."

"Thank you," she said with dignity. "Then may I ask—"

"Surely not why you've been incarcerated," he said with a mocking smile.

"On the contrary, I would like to ask what charges you plan to place against me."

"Any charges would be purely academic since your trial has already taken place," he said flatly.

"My trial?" she gasped. "Without me?"

He nodded. "Perhaps the word trial is a poor word, Mrs. Pollifax—the Intelligence department does not have trials. Let us say instead that a hearing has been held—it took a number of hours, which is why I am so late—and you were quite fairly represented, Mrs. Pollifax."

"Indeed?" she said coldly. "And by whom?"

"By Lieutenant Cevdet Suleiman."

She said indignantly, "I've never met a Lieutenant Suleiman, nor has any such man spoken to me, so that I fail to see how he could represent me. This was doubtless a recommendation of Dr. Belleaux?"

Mr. Piskapos beamed. "It is interesting to hear you

mention Dr. Belleaux's name," he said. "Supposing you tell me how you happen to know Dr. Belleaux."

"What time is it?"

"Five o'clock." He leaned across the desk and displayed his wrist watch to her in case she doubted him.

Mrs. Pollifax hesitated and then nodded. If it was five o'clock in the afternoon then Magda was either safe or not safe, either landing in London or stalled hopelessly in Istanbul. In any case Carstairs could be left out of the picture: the important thing was to place Dr. Belleaux squarely *in* the picture. "Very well," she said, and began to speak of her arrival in Istanbul to help a friend who had appealed to her for aid by cablegram. "Her name," she said carefully, "was Magda Ferenci-Sabo."

If Mr. Piskapos was startled he did not show it; his eyes remained fixed inscrutably upon the blotter on his desk, he did not even blink.

Thus encouraged, Mrs. Pollifax plunged ahead to describe the events of the past four days. She left out very little except the names of Madrali, the Inglescus, and Sandor. When she had finished Mr. Piskapos flicked off the tape recorder.

"Thank you, Mrs. Pollifax," he said simply.

She found this annoyingly casual. She said, "Thank you for what? The truth? Lies? You don't believe what I've said about Dr. Belleaux?"

At her question he looked up, surprised. "Oh yes."

Jarred, she said, "Yes what?"

He smiled. "Perhaps I should tell you now that Dr. Belleaux is also in this prison—but not as a guest of our police this time. He was captured and booked only an hour after you arrived here, and he is here as a prisoner charged with espionage and treason." He smiled wryly. "At the hearing it was decided—because of this, and because of your work in exposing Dr. Belleaux—that Ferenci-Sabo be allowed to continue unmolested to London."

"Magda is safe?" gasped Mrs. Pollifax.

He said gravely, "We could have stopped her, you understand, but in this particular case the Biblical eye for an eye seemed just. In time, all of her information will be shared with my government, and in turn we have—Dr. Belleaux, as Lieutenant Suleiman pointed out to us."

"This lieutenant," began Mrs. Pollifax.

"However, for the safety of everyone concerned," continued Mr. Piskapos, "we have thought it best that if Alice Dexter White goes free, Magda Ferenci-Sabo must die. Die firmly, and publicly." He drew a sheet of paper from under his blotter. "Perhaps you would be interested in the news release we have prepared for the voice wire services?"

Mrs. Pollifax glanced impatiently at a report of Magda Ferenci-Sabo's death. Piskapos was saying, "You will of course wish to send a cable of reassurance to your superior, Mr. Carstairs, in Washington."

At hearing Carstairs' name spoken Mrs. Pollifax nearly choked on the fig that she had at last begun to eat. "You know—about Mr. Carstairs?" she gasped.

Piskapos laughed. "Obviously it is time that you met Cevdet," he said. He leaned back and smiled at Mrs. Pollifax. "I must explain to you that Lieutenant Suleiman had been lately involved in following a man who entered Turkey illegally, Mrs. Pollifax, and who took a job as valet in the employ of a most noted gentleman in Istanbul—to spy on that gentleman, we thought. The name of the man whom Lieutenant Suleiman was keeping under surveillance was Stefan Mihailic, and the gentleman who gave him employment is Dr. Guillaume Belleaux."

Mrs. Pollifax's eyes widened in surprise. "Dr. Belleaux!"

"Which may explain to you," continued Mr. Piskapos dryly, "how it was that Lieutenant Suleiman happened to be watching Dr. Belleaux's house last Monday night when two strangers rode up in a van containing a corpse, proceeded to burglarize Dr. Belleaux's house and then to carry out a half-conscious woman! Without consulting his superiors—but the man is a genius, of course—Lieutenant Suleiman decided that he must follow you in whatever conveyance he could put his hands on and discover what on earth you were up to. He had no idea who you or Ferenci-Sabo were until—alas—it was far too late." Piskapos smiled. "He seems to have acquired the utmost respect for you, Mrs. Pollifax, a respect, I might add, which my government now shares completely."

He leaned over and said into the intercom, "Send in Cevdet, please."

"I am bewildered," admitted Mrs. Pollifax. "I may be overtired but I simply don't understand."

Mr. Piskapos beamed at her reassuringly. "You will have plenty of time to understand. Lieutenant Suleiman has arranged a party for you all tonight in Ankara . . . for you, the young man Colin, Mr. Ramsey and Dmitri—who are already in Ankara now—and I believe something was mentioned of a pretty young woman from Yozgat. But Lieutenant Suleiman will tell you more of this. Ah, come in, Cevdet, come in!"

The door had opened. A figure in dazzling white linen stood there, a figure vaguely familiar and yet—paradoxically—utterly strange to Mrs. Pollifax. Black hair. A thin stripe of a moustache across the upper lip. Dazzling white teeth. Broad shoulders. This was an incredibly handsome man. Then he moved, and Mrs. Pollifax started. Dimly she remembered thinking—was it only a few days ago?—that even if he shaved and bathed she would recognize him because of his vitality, that bounding step and wonderful zest for life.

"Sandor!" she cried.

Mr. Piskapos stood up and said with a smile, "I would like you to meet Lieutenant Cevdet Suleiman, Mrs. Pollifax, of Turkish Intelligence."

Sandor laughed delightedly. "What the hell, eh, Mrs. Pollifax?" he said, and bounded forward to kiss her heartily on each cheek.